A Field Guide to Reality

Joanna Kavenna

riverrun

First published in Great Britain in 2016 by riverrun
This paperback edition published in 2017 by

r

riverrun

An imprint of

Quercus Editions Limited
Carmelite House
50 Victoria Embankment
London EC4Y 0DZ

An Hachette UK company

A CIP catalogue record for this book is available
from the British Library

PB ISBN 978 1 78087 232 2
EBOOK ISBN 978 1 78429 311 6

10 9 8 7 6 5 4 3 2 1

Design by Andrew Barker
Printed and bound in Great Britain by Clays Ltd, St Ives plc

*This book may at times bear some relation
to the historical facts*

. . .

This is invariably coincidental

. . .

In Memory of
DMG (1945–2014)
and
CPR (1943–2015)

ATQUE IN PERPETUUM
. . .
AVE ATQUE VALE

Dramatis Personæ

Plato (*c.* 429–*c.* 347 BC)
Ironist, chatterbox, inventor of Socrates.

Aristotle (384–322 BC)
Obsessive list-maker, had the ear of a great king.

Robert Grosseteste (*c.* 1175–1253)
Futurologist, wizard, mind-bender.

Roger Bacon (*c.* 1214–1294)
Faustian sorcerer, conversed with devils.

Alhazen (*c.* 965–1040)
Arabian scholar, declared himself mad. Observed flying dust.

Lydia Cassavetes (1975–)
Archivist of Hypatia.

Hypatia (*c.* 350–415)
Neoplatonist, genius. Murdered by a Christian mob.

Barnes Martin (date of birth unknown)
Alchemist. Possibly the Comte de St Germain.
Or Fulcanelli.

Isaac Newton (1642–1727)
Called himself Jehovah, the Holy One. Occultist.

Iris McConnell (1980—)
Believes that the present does not exist.

John Locke (1632–1704)
Argued that we are inherently blank.

Lord Priddy (date of birth unknown)
Fan of psychotropic drugs and cricket.

Caspar Overson (1958—)
Believes that everything must be more Ψ.

Albert Einstein (1879–1955)
Found that reality remained mysterious, despite everything.

Table of Contents

Prologue

On 23 January 1216, a double rainbow is seen on Port Meadow, Oxford. It is formed of two vast arches, which span the sky. The feet of the arches are planted at the centre of the meadow, and rise beyond the medieval town. The colours are perfectly rendered: the brightness is overwhelming.

At this time, in line with the teachings of Aristotle, it is believed that rainbows derive from the reflection, by clouds, of the sun. The colours are caused by the dimming effect of clouds.

Gazing at the rainbow, people are in raptures and generally believe that God has presented them with a sign.

After the flood, God sent a rainbow to Noah, as a sign that humanity was forgiven.

There has been no flood, though this city is surrounded by water. Two rivers circumnavigate the place, and merge to the south.

Whispers emanate across the meadow marsh . . .

If this is a sign, then what does it mean?

o o o

The Chronicler
of Alhazen

Life in thirteenth-century Oxford is hard and dangerous. The homicide rate exceeds modern-day Bogota. Each year for every hundred monks attending the university (all students must be in religious orders), three are murdered, fifteen die of dysentery, and twenty-six run away to London.

The gates of the town close at dusk.

Walter Raleigh has not yet visited the New World and there are no potatoes or tobacco. The staple foods are bread, porridge and gruel. Meat is expensive and only the rich are assured of a reliable supply. Because of the Eucharist, bread is endowed with particular status and is consumed regularly, incessantly –

With deleterious physical effects and perhaps to the general despond of all:

MENU PRIX FIXE

STARTER:
Bread

MAIN:
Parsimonious cuts of meat with Ample Bread

DESSERT:
Bread Pudding

The sallow streets of medieval Oxford are riddled with people in varying states of acute and even chronic indigestion, trying to walk off the latest incursion of
Bread
As the first Chancellor of the university, Robert Grosseteste presides over a series of monastic Halls –

Worm Hall
Cat Hall
Bull Hall
Hare Hall
Unicorn Hall
Woodcock Hall
Nightingale Hall
Eagle Hall
Sparrow Hall
Hawk Hall
Ape Hall
Beefe Hall
Perilous Hall
Kepeharm Hall
Aristotle Hall
Nun's Hall
Pie Hall

Grosseteste is also known as Grossteste, Gros-
test, Grostet, Grosthead, Grouthead, Gros-
tede, Greatheade, Grosteheved, Greateheved,
Grosehede, Grokede, and Goschede. In this
era, spellings are not fixed and the creative
possibilities are endless. Yet Grosseteste of the
mutable and at times suggestive name has more
pressing matters to deal with. He is transfixed
by mysteries. How do we see what we see? How
do we know that what we see is real? Besides,
he cannot fix himself in time. He ricochets
from one continent to another, across the
centuries. He wonders at times if he is mad.

The eye is a lantern, says Empedocles the Greek and Grosseteste tries to catch the rest of his words . . .

As when a man, thinking to go out into the wintry night, makes ready a light, a flame of blazing fire . . .

Now Grosseteste sees Plato, surrounded by students and acolytes. Plato is explaining that light is a mixture of the inner fire of the eye, and the fire of the sun . . . *The fire within us, which is akin to the daylight, flows pure, smooth and dense through the eyes . . .*

This coalesces with daylight, says Plato, to form one uniform body . . . *Its uniformity becomes sympathetic . . .*

Grosseteste hides in the shade of an olive tree, he watches the people watching Plato. And even as he falters on the brink of a further realisation – he moves again, drifts through a few brief ages and now he is at the Lyceum with Aristotle.

Aristotle says: *the eye does not emit light, instead light enters the eye from the world beyond.*

The eye is Not a torch, a burning brand, striking the world with its radiant light. Plato's theories are ludicrous.

The acolytes shift, they are uncertain.

Aristotle looks up – he sees Grosseteste nodding in the shadows – he is moving towards the cleric when – dark clouds obliterate the sun. Darkness spreads across the strange dream of Robert Grosseteste and the sky turns black, the DARK AGES are upon him.

This always happens, Grosseteste remembers, just when Aristotle is on the verge of speaking to him –

The mind cannot imagine such a prospect – he wonders –

And in the darkness he wonders if he is dying –

The DARK AGES are upon him

When dawn breaks, Grosseteste finds he is in Cairo. It is the eleventh century.

Though he is a metaphysical wraith, he sweats.

The city is kiln-hot, the streets are fired by a harsh sun.

Grosseteste hurries from one shadow to another.

Sunlight glares onto the white houses.

Horses clatter past him. And everything is swirled around in dust that blows in from the desert.

Ibn al-Haytham, known to posterity as Alhazen, is under house arrest. He was recently employed by Al-Hākim bi Amr Allāh, sixth ruler of the Fatimid caliphate, to control the flooding of the Nile. After a relatively short period of enquiry, it became quite apparent that Alhazen could not, in any discernible sense, achieve this task. As Al-Hākim was not renowned for his forgiving nature, Alhazen was forced to proclaim himself Mad. The defence saved his life, and yet now he is confined to his house. He can no longer ride across the desert at twilight, observing the rising of the silver moon. He can no longer venture to Mesopotamia, where he studied Aristotle in his youth. Despite such physical limitations, Alhazen embarks upon a Quest For Truth . . .

In a dark room – light that enters through HOLES is visible in the Dust that Fills the Air –

With these layers of shining dust, Alhazen tries to prove that light travels in straight lines only.

In this City of Dust, there are ample opportunities for Alhazen to test his theory . . .

In the dust storms that choke . . .

The dust that drifts onto the pages as Alhazen writes – Dust sparkling like diamonds.

Beyond, the smoke, dreams, the dead swirling, the clouds and dust, ashes, the lights that flame and glitter in the skies.

Robert Grosseteste considers the dust that floats in the air and renders light visible –

Is Light a material substance? says Grosseteste to himself. Ages have passed around him and he has drifted back to

Oxford. His mind is addled today
and his stomach aches. The sky is
deep and swart. In this hall, they
choose between warmth and light;
there is no glass across the window.

Draughts oppress him, make him
cough and shiver.

Though his room is filled with pale
light, though the lighted dust swirls, he
tries to remember –

A dream of light?

Grosseteste presents an epistemology of light, a
metaphysics of light, an etiology of light, and a theology
of light. He describes the birth of the universe in an explo-
sion, and a further crystallisation of matter. All creation
emerges from an expanding – and contracting – sphere
of light.

And the Lord said, 'Let there be Light!'

A few days or aeons later, Grosseteste is at dinner again.
He abhors the draughts that swirl through the echoing
hall. The monks sit quietly except for Grosseteste and his
companions at the highest table, who are arguing –

Hunger, weariness, general fret and besides they do not
agree about Universals –

The company includes:

> Roger Bacon – The Marvellous Doctor
> Adam Marsh – The Illustrious Doctor
> John Duns Scotus – The Subtle Doctor
> William of Ockham – The Invincible Doctor

Dining, alas, on bread.
In this shadowy echoing hall –
Roger Bacon explains –

> *How gunpowder might be created*
> *The possibility of a flying machine*
> *How to design a magnifying glass*

Bacon, too, is transfixed by the mysteries of light, and perception, and how the eye sees anything at all. He has created, he suggests, a strange device which displays shadows against a wall. When Bacon first presents his spectacle of light and shade he terrifies his audience. Figures leer, gargantuan, menacing – the crowd shuffles backwards, screams.

As night falls, Bacon walks through the streets and scarcely notices the shifty cut-throats emerging from the shadows. He looks at the darkening sky and remembers the Islamic scholar Al-Kindi, who thought that every creature in the universe is a source of radiation and the universe itself a vast network of forces. These forces, or species, are often not visible. But light is.

Thus, Bacon realises, Light is the most extraordinary and most intriguing of all realities, because it is as if the Wind became visible. Or, as if Thought streamed in colours across the sky.

For his scholarly pursuits and unrivalled experimentation, Bacon is quite naturally accused of necromancy and consorting with the Devil . . . In this he joins a long line of visionaries accused by their enemies of treachery or heresy –

Socrates, disposed of by a state that found him profoundly irritating . . .
Boethius, who was imprisoned and later murdered by King Theodric
    the Great . . .
Galileo Galilei, oppressed and silenced by the Church . . .
Countless unknown wise women, drowned or burnt.

Also at dinner is John Duns Scotus who produces rigorous and munificent works of learning until he is accidentally buried alive.

His servant, who is fully aware that Duns Scotus has a tendency to catatonia, is unfortunately absent when his master collapses and doctors are summoned. Thus Duns Scotus is pronounced dead, and cast into the ground . . .

Later, William of Ockham –
    The Invincible Doctor –
    explains that mathematical entities are Not Real –
    and lends his name to the notion of Occam's Razor. Put simply, this is the proposition that the Simplest Theory is the Best.
    But THEN
    William of Ockham creates a Massive Cataclysm . . .
    In his dream, Grosseteste stirs, and calls out NO NO –
he foresees the schism, he can hardly prevent it.
    Ideas will flow and spawn new ideas and then –

Ockham is sitting in another cold Oxford hall. A fire flickering in the grate, shadows dancing on the walls. It is 1321.
    He has read Grosseteste's work and the works of

Roger Bacon, and Duns Scotus, the buried man, and he
has mused liberally on the questions of:

How do we know what it is that we See?
And does perception create the world, or is it there before
    us, present and perpetual?

When the realisation comes, Ockham is so shocked, he
clasps his hands to his ears, hoping thereby he might
deafen himself to his own thoughts.

He begins to tremble –

METAPHYSICAL UNIVERSALS ARE NOT REAL

These abstracts, all the forms of Plato, the grandiose notion
that there are universal versions of each flawed aspect of
the mortal world, the universal forms of Light –

Do not Exist.

A scene of general horror at the Great Table as the scholars pause, knives aloft –

William of Ockham denies that there are perpetual elements that unify all creation . . .

Instead he believes –

That everything is unlike everything else, and there can
be no synthesis . . .

(Except – he says, nervously, with an eye on the Pope –
In God.)

The Pope excommunicates him anyway . . .

Threadbare and no longer quite as invincible as before,
Ockham devotes himself to scholarship.

(And calls the Pope a heretic.)
No universals.
No whole.
Reality changes . . .

◦ ◦ ◦

11

A Field Guide
to Reality

Many centuries later it was 2016 and I was a few decades into my current lifespan. I was spending my time in Oxford. There are many worse places. Conditions had significantly improved since the thirteenth century and the trials of Grosseteste. Bread was still abundant, but was now treated with suspicion, as a decadent substance. On these grounds, some people refused even to consume it. The city was glinting and prosperous. Great lines of traffic snaked across the bridges, passing beneath the spires and gargoyles. The north of the city, mere pastureland at the time of Grosseteste, was now full of Victorian mansions, overlooked by further gargoyles, in architectural homage to vanished ages. Intended originally as family

accommodation for married dons, they were now owned
by stockbrokers and bankers, interspersed with a few
oligarchs and former tyrants.

I lived in a small rented room in a little house in East
Oxford, the workers' regions of the nineteenth-century
city, now colonised by students and by all those dons who
could no longer afford to live in the North. I was neither a
student, nor a don; I worked in a café and occasionally did
some research work at the university. In the evenings I sat
in the Great Library, another significant medieval edifice,
and studied the history of the city. When I arrived back
at my small rented room, and slept, the words I had read

that evening informed my dreams, taking me back to dusty
Cairo and even to the mud⸝plains of medieval Oxford.
The hawkers and criminals, waiting with their knives. I
was biting my hands and shouting when I woke. The walls
of my room were thin and I could hear my landlady mov⸝
ing around, the floorboards creaking under her feet.

I realised then the phone was ringing. I had fallen asleep
earlier, a book in my hand. I glanced at my watch and saw
it was only midnight.

I picked up the phone and heard a man saying, 'Is that
Eliade Jencks? I'm very sorry to disturb you.'

I struggled to the window and looked out at the street
which was – blanked out. A dense mist coiled around the
yellow streetlights. The voice was saying – 'I'm a colleague
of Professor Solete. I believe he was a friend of yours?'

So I knew Solete was dead.

Why else do people call you at midnight?

When I looked at my watch I saw the date was January
the fourth. Deep within the phone, this voice was telling
me how sorry he was. How it had been swift. Painless.
Solete had greeted the porter and checked his pigeonhole.
Then he had gone up to his room as usual and –

'He didn't suffer.'

'How do *you* know?' I said.

'I mean, it was very sudden. As if he was hit by a
thunderbolt.'

In the mist, the houses had blurred into a single line of
bricks. His name was Anthony Yorke, he told me, and
he was a historian of ideas at Solete's college, Nightingale
Hall. He had been placed in charge of Solete's literary

estate, by order of the college. I imagined illustrious
fellows, like venerable birds, huddled in a feathery cluster
in a wood-panelled room, holding fountain pens in their
shivering beaks.

'We'd like you to come over to the college tomorrow.
There's something about the estate that we need to discuss.'

'We?'

The venerable birds.

'The fellows.'

I imagined Solete as a boy, adored by his mother and
father; I saw him at every phase of his life, rushing through
his youth, vigorous and committed, falling in love, marry-
ing a brilliant scholar he later mourned so deeply, Asta
Rose. And all the further years and decades of Solete's life.
The days must have seemed continuous, and yet now his
lifespan was complete.

Anthony Yorke was saying that there was a box in
Solete's room, with *For Eliade* on the lid. This interested
me, because Solete had mentioned a grand project on a
few occasions, something he aimed to complete – before
he died. It was, he claimed, his life's work, and its central
themes were reality and truth; or, how it is that we see what
we see, and how we know whether what we see is real. It
was, he explained, one more mark on the great page of
philosophical enquiry. He refused to tell me anything else,
except that he jokingly referred to it as *A Field Guide to
Reality*.

'Among his papers he explains that the box can only be
opened by you,' Yorke was saying. 'My colleagues and I
wondered if you might come to Solete's rooms in college,
first thing tomorrow?'

We haggled briefly over a feasible time, and how I had to work, and how the scholarly birds had to impart their wisdom to the young, then Yorke said he would look forward to our meeting. He was wildly over-excited because he wanted to open the box of treasure.

We said goodbye.

I was thinking of Solete and his decades of enterprise, and I was still trying to register the fact of his death. I kept thinking of questions I had failed to ask him. I had always intended to sit down with him and interview him, about his childhood, and his youth, and his further thoughts on existence and reality. He had been effortlessly erudite; I had always loved to talk to him. I went back to bed and tried to apprehend the truth: that he had descended into the realm of shadows, or the vaporous terrain of nowhere. A few times I was nearly asleep when, suddenly, I jolted awake in pure existential panic, afraid of the eternality of death and even about to scream. The night was viscous; darkened mist swirled at the windows, as if the air was charred. At some point and despite my overall perplexity I must have fallen asleep because I dreamed I was talking to Solete. He was there and he was telling me he was dead. I said I was so sorry, and I was so entirely sorry, I wanted to cry again.

'We are made of stardust,' he said. 'Isn't that strange?'

I woke and the sky was silver-white. I couldn't work out what I had dreamed and what I had remembered. I went downstairs and turned on all the lights.

By nine a.m. I was running down the Cowley Road, towards Nightingale Bridge. The whole place was covered in whitewash, someone had hurled it over the trees, so they looked petrified. Everyone was walking so fast, they kept colliding in the mist. And in the doorways of the shops people said, 'Mist? Ridiculous! So cold. Soaks your brain.

You can't think clearly. You go deaf. It's like wool in your ears.'

A man with a phone at his mouth, keeping pace alongside me: 'Becca's taken the car but she'll never get anywhere in this. Perpetual misery.'

I passed Nun's Hall, the first women's college – they used to chain the women to the furniture, so they didn't get distracted by Sin.

People round me wiped their hands, puffing at each other. 'So awful, so thick and wet.'

Vapour, it gets you in the end. The body is almost entirely water. The last thing you need is to get whirled around in wet air. You might dissolve!

Now I was passing Hawk Plain, with Café Woodcock to my right – the windows slimy with condensation. Bodies moving inside. In Kepeharm Hall they train the priests. *For Thine is the Kingdom.*

KNOWN FACTS ABOUT
NIGHTINGALE HALL

Nightingale Hall – founded by Sir Richard Black (1492–1567), who was Master of the Merchant Taylor Company and Lord Mayor of London. He was a supporter of the Catholic Queen Mary Tudor, daughter of Henry VIII. At least, he said he was in public. His inner thoughts were, of course, private. Yet he officially backed Mary; he sat by while the Queen burnt all her heretics and for this certain propping up of the establishment, while it was, briefly, the establishment, he was rewarded with land in the centre of Oxford, a fine location near St Giles (pie shops, a church), fields and countryside to the north. The college was founded to support Mary's strong-minded efforts in religious conversion and when Mary's soul left her body amen a few fellows had to flee, including Richard Cartwright, the famous poet. ('Sort the roses from the weeds . . . for time is all a-fleeting . . .')

Black's widow died without issue, as they say, and so she left all her wealth to Nightingale Hall.

Nightingale Hall has a beautiful setting on Nightingale Bridge, which spans the River Cherwell. The College is known for its May Day celebrations, when the choristers of Nightingale School stand on the top of the college tower, and sing like angels to herald the advent of Spring. There are gargoyles all along the front of Nightingale Hall, peering down at Unicorn Street. Beasts spouting water, men snarling in agony, and two young women, asleep.

Through the mist, a hallowed quad or two. The Porter, a saturnine figure of indeterminate age, told me how sorry he was about Professor Solete.

'A major gap in our lives,' he said. Then he went back to reading the paper.

But then, what else could he do?

Solete's room was on staircase XXIII. The door opened onto the expected scene: antique furniture, learned detritus. Three scholars, displayed in armchairs. It turned out I had met Anthony Yorke before, at a party. I was disoriented when he rang at midnight, and failed to make the connection. Besides, my mind was on other things. He seemed to be experiencing a similar moment of confusion, mingled perhaps with slight dismay. But, who can tell what others are thinking?

'Duncan Saunders's party,' I said to him. 'That's where we met, I mean.'

'Yes, yes, of course,' he said, politely. 'Are you a friend of his?'

Duncan Saunders makes things from wood. Assembles them in public spaces. Calls them 'happenings' so no one will judge him too harshly.

'This is Anthony Yorke,' Duncan had said, standing back to reveal a big man, with white-blond hair. Running out of a broken marriage, though I didn't know that. 'He's new.'

Hand out, clammy fingers.

'Nightingale Hall,' he said. Christ, I thought, an academic.

Nod politely now, recover later.

'And you?' he said.

'No no, I really don't do much,' I said.

One thing I've learned, is not to tell anyone anything. It seems by far the best option. So many people just unwind the whole thing, the moment you ask them a single question. Then you get all this stuff, life detail, well, it's cumbersome, yards and yards of it, mile upon mile, unravelled towards you, until you're stumbling under the weight. So I say as little as possible. Damage limitation. No one can hold you to account, no one can judge you. Yet, Anthony lacked my defensive restraint. He twitched, and then he spoke. He was working on something so esoteric I'd blinked a hundred times before he'd got halfway through it. 'A potted summary,' he said. I couldn't imagine what the extended version sounded like. You'd have to sit down. Nurse a triple whisky. Then you might stand a chance of enduring it . . .

'I study ancient theories of Light,' he said. 'Rainbows, for example. How many colours does a rainbow have?'

'Is that a trick question?'

He laughed. 'You need a lot of time, for this sort of thing,' he said. 'The whole world. Your entire being. You have to pick it apart slowly.'

'Why?' I said.

'Because . . .' He paused. 'Well,' he said. 'You pick it apart, and then you do it to yourself, demolish yourself, and then you think the rest of the world will come too . . . but it doesn't. Everyone else just sits there . . . Happy, talking about verisimilitude. Like a pack of madmen. Women too.'

'You're just an elitist,' I said. 'And don't pretend to me you care what women do.'

That just set him off on another paragraph. Perhaps it was seven pages, without a pause, that sort of thing. What? Another fifteen, did I want a thesis?

'OK, you care deeply,' I said. 'It's moving how you care.'

Did I want a drink? We stood apart, we talked about the crowd. He'd come from London, he told me. All the way, to Oxford, to a small room at Nightingale Hall. There to discuss—

No no, he was going to tell me again –

'Really, it's OK,' I said. 'I believe you . . .'

This morning, he put his hand out again, and I shook it. We were both being very formal and serious. Behind him: a tumbling array of books, papers, tattered sofas, sketchy carpet, curtains half-drawn across aged windows — then beyond — the whiteness.

'My colleagues,' said Anthony. 'Sasha Petrovka and Patrick O'Donovan . . . Patrick teaches philosophy, and Sasha is our professor of Ancient Greek. We've all been tasked with administering the estate.' I nodded towards a pair of real flinty sticks. Folding their flinty limbs into armchairs. Sasha Petrovka dressed all in black. Black gloves pulled up to her elbows. Long black skirt, black boots. Long face, long black hair. Sharp angles. Patrick O'Donovan in generic don. You couldn't get much more don than that. Tweed jacket, mustard scarf, burgundy cords. Such a clash of shades and tones, as if he was daring you to protest.

But this is the Winchonian Blag, did you not know, you frightful peasant?

'This is Solete's friend and collaborator, Eliade Jencks,' said Anthony. So they nodded and offered their condolences, told me how wonderful Solete had been. Anthony was pouring tea with a trembling hand. An untucked shirt, debased formality, an ancient suit.

'Well, so, as we know, Solete was working for decades, with Asta Rose, and then alone after her death, on his great work . . . Solete was a philosopher, emphasis on the ancient world but curious and erudite in general, and Asta was a cosmologist, I think you could say, and they always said they encompassed past, present, future. By mistake.'

'Theirs?' said Petrovka.

'I mean, happy coincidence. But really — they laboured away and then Asta died, er — I think it was . . . ?' Yorke turned to me.

'Two decades ago,' I said.

'Absolutely.' They all looked sorry again. 'So, Solete continued on his own. He continued, for a very long time.'

'He said he was just preparing the final elements,' I said.

'He was always deliberately vague,' said Yorke.

Everyone was quiet for a moment – O'Donovan with his tragic-comic gnawed fingers and Anthony, leaning awkwardly against the desk. Petrovka was slumped in her chair, apparently deep in thought – yet I imagined that under her half-closed eyes she was watching like a hawk.

'Well, Dr Churchwood's pretty adamant,' said O'Donovan. 'He wants it for the college library.'

'Someone should take charge of this,' said Petrovka.

There was a painting above the mantelpiece, of the Thames as it meanders through Port Meadow. Layered hills reflected in the cold blue water. The room smelled of laundered handkerchiefs, pipe smoke, with a background trace of sherry. Solete once told me that he regarded his college as the home of lost causes. The young, so urgent, hustling towards a point they believed to be fixed and which would nonetheless recede, so it was always ahead of them. And the old, who were – said Solete – mainly glad they were still residual and present. His room was riddled with objects – books of course, stacked randomly, with scant attention to gravity, tumbling into dusty piles if you moved too swiftly.

There were photographs of Asta Rose who once had abundant silver hair and an expression of mocking enquiry. There were cards from so many dusty ancient scholars, an exhibition of writing styles. The place had lapsed into incoherence, and yet recently it had been explained by the presence of Solete. It seemed impossible that he was no longer alive. I rebelled against the fact; I found it reprehensible. The death of others rids you briefly of egotism, because you focus not, at all, on your own obsolescence – which will come – but on theirs, which has already occurred. It is peaceful agony, to mourn in this way, because at least it is agony focused on a single element. It is when you fall into mourning for everyone, humanity, the whole fragile fleeting edifice – that sends you mad!

Meanwhile, two stickle-backed velociraptors had come to inspect the rubble. I was not certain I trusted O'Donovan or Petrovka.

Anthony emerged, carrying a small chest, bearing it towards me like a votive offering.

He set it down on the desk, amidst tonnes of discarded paper, and fountain pens, and a Bavarian ornamental clock in the shape of a chalet. On the top was written, in Solete's sloping hand, *For Eliade*.

'In essence, it's the property of the college,' said O'Donovan.

'That's not true,' said Anthony. 'Look at what is written on the lid.'

'For Eliade to open, for the college to guard, perhaps,' said O'Donovan. He tried to smile charmingly, but his mouth was too wide, too lopsided, so the expression looked more like a sneer.

'It belonged to Solete. And he has given it to Eliade, after his death,' said Anthony.

'College rooms. Property intrinsic,' said O'Donovan.

'No remote precedent for that.'

'Well, in the case of sensitive objects, it might be

possible to invoke, some kind of property – I mean – he
was insured by the college. Wasn't he?'

That really got Yorke roaming around the place.
Knocking books over, sluicing down a cup of tea. 'No,
the bloody hell, I mean? Actually when something belongs
to someone they can do whatever they like. I give it away,
so it's not mine anymore. Especially if I'm dead.'

'Well, it's a quandary,' said O'Donovan. 'I've got
Churchwood hopping around – I saw him yesterday –
and then it turned out it was bequeathed to this random
stranger, he was almost crying with frustration – his big
moment – great discovery – the Solete papers, the complete
work, the man is inconsolable and if Solete wasn't already
dead he'd be off to lynch him.'

'But it's the request of the deceased,' said Anthony
again. 'There can be no possible argument.'

'But did Solete make it absolutely clear? Is the document
signed?' said Sasha Petrovka, joining in. 'Can we see it?'

'You don't want to get Solete haunting you,' said
Anthony, mainly to Petrovka. But she didn't care. You
could tell. She would happily tell the ghost of Solete to
stop menacing her and she would affright that poor shade
all the way back to the underworld.

'He won't haunt anyone,' said Petrovka. 'He wasn't that
sort.'

'Really, you're certain of the dispositions and taxonomies of the afterlife?' said Anthony. 'So astounding.
Certainty about the invisible . . .'

'Anyway, there are distinctions. The peaceful dead and
the raving ghouls,' said O'Donovan. By now, he was biting his fingers. 'I mean, he was paid by the college for five

millennia or whatever it was and this is what he did. And so surely the college has some share of it? And isn't there an obligation to keep it safe?'

'Whatever *it* is,' I said.

They all looked at me.

'The irony is,' I said. 'You don't even know.'

There was a pause, and then O'Donovan sighed, and tried to lift the lid of the box. No one expected it to open, and, as expected, it didn't. He sighed again.

'Where's the key?' said Petrovka.

'Well, he sent it to you, didn't he?' said O'Donovan, turning to me.

'No, he didn't.'

'Surely, he did,' said Petrovka. They were both looking at me as if I were hiding something. But I really didn't have a key.

'What about the porter?' I said. 'Or some other practical person, with a crowbar?'

'Oh, yes,' said Anthony. 'Yes, a good point.'

'And they say academics lack common sense,' said O'Donovan. 'Here we are, the serried professionals of a supposedly eminent college, and we require assistance in our deductive processes from a—'

'Waitress,' I said.

He waved a hand at me, as if he hadn't liked to sully me, or indeed himself, with such a word. Anthony was speaking into the phone. That elicited, after a brief pause, the lugubrious porter from the lodge. He came in and for a while he dolefully smacked the lock with a hammer. 'Very cheap mechanism,' he said. The lock fell apart.

Even Lady Petrovka stood. There was a pause while

we all looked at the box. Then I lifted the lid, as everyone leaned forward.

'Is it?' said Petrovka, an accidental exhalation. 'Could it?' But it wasn't. It couldn't.

The box was empty. There was no book, and no grand and final theory of Reality. No *Field Guide*. Nothing but air and dust. The absence of anything had a significant effect on everyone. The anticlimax first conveyed the porter from the room, pursued by Yorke, who wanted to thank him. Then everyone reconvened at the chest and marked their astonishment at first with total silence and then with rage and mutual accusation.

'Where the bloody hell,' said O'Donovan, 'is it?'

'It isn't here,' said Petrovka. 'That is all. And if not here, it is somewhere else. And thus, it can be found.'

'Have you already moved it?' said O'Donovan, to Anthony, who looked irritated and made a noise to indicate that of course he hadn't.

'Why would I?' he added. His cheeks were slightly flushed.

'Well then, what the bloody hell has happened to it?' said O'Donovan.

'Calm down, Patrick. Your career *will* survive, you know,' said Petrovka. 'It'll limp on. Churchwood won't actually fire you.'

'No, I'll tell him to fire you, instead,' said O'Donovan. They looked at each other with naked mutual loathing, and then Anthony said, 'Solete must have changed his mind, just before he died, and moved it.'

'Nonsense, he wasn't like that,' said O'Donovan. 'Some bastard has taken it.'

'Well, which bastard?' said Petrovka. 'That's the only important question.'

'What will you do with it, when you find it?' I said. I was genuinely curious. Petrovka gave me a considering look, then went to sit on her chair again. Had you arrived into the room at that moment, you would have seen Petrovka, apparently at ease, and O'Donovan with his head almost in the fire and Anthony looking blank and worried and me – I don't know what I was doing. I could hardly feel the loss of something I never expected to have. But I was annoyed, that the box with my name on it was so conspicuously empty.

'So, I assume no one has any objections to Eliade taking away this box,' said Anthony.

'Christ no,' said Petrovka. She stood, putting on her gloves. She gestured vaguely at the clock. 'Take anything you like. I should be off.'

'Oh well, nice to meet you,' I said.

'Oh yes, you too,' she said. 'Intriguing business.'

Petrovka went away. I imagined her strolling down the corridor, dismissing the whole mess. An old professor, who went insane, and thought he had plumbed the depths of the universe, and who, instead, left a vacant box! And the poor woman who trooped into the college, expecting to receive a great prize, and went away with nothing. It was an anecdote for High Table, at least.

Now O'Donovan was muttering about a book he had to write, and the draconian regulations of the library. Just too many students as well, he was saying.

'Eliade,' he said, shaking my hand. He talked for a while. He was painstakingly affable. Do hope I didn't

offend, and thanks so much for coming in. Very fond of
Solete. Knew him for years. 'Would you like any other of
his books, effects and so on? A memento or two?'

I told O'Donovan I would be fine. 'Knowing Solete as
I did,' he said, from the doorway, 'I think it was just a joke.
He was essentially a comedian.'

He went away.

Academics! I thought. Yorke was sorting through a pile
of papers on the desk, a series of scraps, with headings like
'The Pinecone' and 'Why the Sky is Black'. They looked
like rough notes, to be incorporated into a final work, or a
vanished book.

'Are you rushing off too?' said Yorke, as I gathered my
coat and scarf.

'I have to go and work, in the café,' I said. 'What about
you?'

Did I want another cup of tea? No no, I really couldn't.

'What will you do, about the book?' he said.

'Well, I don't know.'

'You could search for it in his house?'

'I might, yes.'

'I could help, if you like? Just let me know. My room is
across the quad. The porter will show you. Or, my number – well, just call the college. Anytime – if I can help.'

I thanked him, then I left in a hurry, I really was late.
He waved his hand to me, in an awkward way, and went
back to leaning over the desk.

○ ○ ○

iii

The Tradescantian
Ark

I came to Oxford on the advice of my mother. In those days I really listened to her. Then it became clear, life was not her specialist subject after all. She was clinging on, like anyone else. Like everyone. Spilling out theories. Still, at the time – in the days when her words fell as exhortations from a deity, adamantine, to be obeyed, I heard her saying, 'Thou shalt go to Oxford.' She thought the atmosphere would lift me up, I would be transformed. Osmosis. Or virtuous contagion. I'd catch cleverness, like a desirable malady. All her years of disappointment – erased!

If she'd been rich, then things would have been better, she often said. But she really wasn't. My father, meanwhile, went to a random office, annihilated himself in the required way, head bowed. He was mostly silent – my mother was still raging urgently. She had a piece of paper – This is where you have to work, she said – the Tradescantian Ark Museum – here – Jeremiah Tradescant began it, some time in the remote past and now –

I took the piece of paper – it said:

A Babylonian vest
Eggs from Turkie, one given for a Dragons egge
Easter egges of the Patriarchs of Jerusalem
Two feathers of the Phoenix Tayle
The claw of the bird rock, who is able to trusse an elephant
Dodar from the Island of Mauritius, it is not able to flie being so big
Hares head, with rough horns three inches long
Toad fish and one with prickles
Divers things cut on plum-stones
A cherry stone, upon one side St. George and the Dragon, perfectly
    cut and on the other side eighty-eight emperors' faces

The figure of a man singing and a woman playing on the Lute; the
*   shadow of the worke being David's Psalms in Dutch*
A brazen-balle to warm the nunne's hands
Blood that rained in the Isle of Wight, attested by Sir Jo Oglander
A bracelet made of the thighes of Indian flies

'The original contents of the Tradescantian Ark,' said my
mother. 'Tradescant collected them . . .'

I loved the sound of these words. I wondered what it
would be like to hold such curios, and I thought a great
deal about this man Tradescant and why, and how, he had
amassed them. I learned the list off by heart, and then I
went to see Dr Canterbridge and Professor Roberts. They
were a kindly pair, but I didn't know what to say to them.
Afterwards, I went down the steps of that beautiful place
and I knew I didn't stand a chance. They were tactful as
well, Canterbridge and Roberts, and afterwards they sent me
a kind euphemism, about how I had very nearly won them
over, despite everything, and how they wished me all the best.

So instead I got a job at the Tradescantian Museum café,
in the basement. This museum was on St Giles. I was
running there, passing the blurred features of Pie Hall,
a few gargoyles, swaddled, past the Great Library – so
many books, their pages mottled with age. Normally when
I arrived at the Museum I went upstairs and stared at
Tradescant's Ark, revealed in little glass boxes. But today
I didn't have time. I had to go and serve coffee and ladle
food onto plates and hand them to – anyone. Everyone. As
I rushed into the kitchen the cook was already raging mad.

'Get the stuff out now. It's going cold!'

I went to my allocated place, and started serving.

'Beans sir? Chips or peas?'

Milk with your coffee? Sugar with your beard? Marma⁄
lade with your air of venerable antiquity?

Sir? Sir?

Today there was a persistent theme. Everyone had
something to contribute. 'The mist,' said the woman with
a green pullover and a couple of kids in tow; 'The mist,'
said a pair of students to each other, and how Harry fell
off his bike on the Cowley Road, poor fool . . .

Bevin, the manager, was frantic, he didn't like delays,
he had fifteen plates to serve and his employees were as late
and idle and useless as ever, the food was going cold and
people kept complaining. The mist swirled beyond the
windows, but the room was candle⁄lit, a fire burnt in the
grate. The sun set slowly, the mist was stained orange . . .
purple . . . black. I went to throw some rubbish out, I
stood in the turgid night, listening to the hum of traffic,
I thought of the many dead, tried not to think.

When I looked up, I couldn't see the stars.

I went back inside and as I closed the door behind me
I realised my heart was thumping, I had started to sweat.
But why?

I often found that I was observing the transient residents
of the café, as they rustled papers or waited nervously for
their friends or lovers. It was in this place that I first met
Solete. He had a distinct routine; he came into the café
each morning at eleven a.m. and stayed until the lunchtime
rush began, at one p.m. The café was in an ancient vault
so the noise rolled around like thunder. Solete seemed not
to notice. He had a small notebook and he wrote copious

notes in a crabbed archaic script, something more gothic than copperplate. He wrote quickly and he seemed to be entirely absorbed in his labours.

When you work in a café you are transfixed by the weird routines of regular customers and how in general we cleave to repetitive protocols. Of course your own day is repetitive because the same meals must be served at the same times, and people want coffee and croissants in the mornings and then strangely not in the evenings and they want soup at lunchtime but never at breakfast. The same people emerge at the same time each day, with very slight discrepancies. Then there are the freak occurrences, anomalies that distinguish one small day from the next. The man who weeps loudly in the corner and the old woman who has dyed her hair pink and green, and the boy in the buggy who squawks like a parrot and so on. These interruptions into the general order allow you at least to refer your day into anecdote, so if anyone is kind enough to ask you can say, 'Yes, today a boy squawked like a parrot,' rather than merely oppressing them with ongoing recurrent minutiae that they can imagine anyway.

So Solete was a ritual presence, and yet he was sufficiently odd to be interesting every day. He was thereby intrinsically paradoxical and presumably impossible. Despite his logical unlikelihood he turned up every day, and he was consistent and extraordinary at the same time. Each day I served him two strong coffees and a bowl of porridge and smiled politely, and he was equally polite, or perhaps even more so. We were nothing to each other, of course, except two sides of a Janus head, youth and age, or insignificance and significance, or half-formed failure and

full-formed success and so on. Then my father died. It was
a dreadful shock, and indeed so great was the shock that
no sooner had the hospital wheeled my father away to the
morgue than I collected all his suddenly extraneous belong-
ings and simply took them back to Oxford, and went
into work as usual the following day. I didn't really know
what else to do. Of course, a death brings insane torrents
of bureaucracy, but I couldn't face embarking on them at
first, I was too tired and I couldn't believe they were really
necessary, because, even though I had seen it, watched
life ebb from my own father's eyes, I couldn't believe my
father was actually dead and assumed at times that what
had plainly occurred must be a nightmare from which I
would soon awake. Despite this, all that day I was afflicted
by sudden recollections of my father, lying like an injured
animal on his side, with his eyes half-closed, gasping for
breath, and how this was a peaceful end, I was fortunate,
and he was fortunate, and yet each time it felt as if someone
had stabbed me through the heart. I couldn't stop crying;
all day I served tables with tears running down my face.

People are kind, often, and yet they are busy, always, and
so no one really noticed, and that was fine and even preferable. When I arrived at Solete's table, however, he glanced
up, which was unusual, and noticed me. Of course then I
was embarrassed, and wiped my face and turned abruptly
away. I became very busy, moving cutlery, but then I heard
him saying something which I didn't understand. I asked
him if he was talking to me (or just muttering crazily to
himself) and he said, yes, of course. 'But don't worry,' he
added. 'You're busy, I'll write it down for you. Catullus.'
When I was called away, he nodded at me, and when it

was one p.m. and time for him to depart he walked past
me and handed me a piece of paper.

> *multas per gentes et multa per aequora vectus*
> *advenio has miseras frater ad inferias*
> *ut te postremo donarem munere mortis*
> *et mutam nequiquam alloquerer cinerem*
> *quandoquidem fortuna mihi tete abstulit ipsum*
> *heu miser indigne frater adempte mihi*
> *nunc tamen interea haec prisco quae more parentum*
> *tradita sunt tristi munere ad inferias*
> *accipe fraterno multum manantia fletu*
> *atque in perpetuum frater ave atque vale*

Which he had considerately translated for me, as there
wasn't the slightest hope of me translating it myself:

> *Through many nations and over many seas have I travelled,*
> *To you, brother, for these wretched funeral rites*
> *so that I might bring you a final tribute*
> *and speak in vain to silent ash,*
> *Since Fortune has carried you away from me*
> *Alas, poor brother, taken away from me,*
> *Leaving me to honour you with the old rites*
> *As it is from generation to generation*
> *Take from my hands these sad gifts as I weep brotherly tears*
> *And forever, brother, hail and farewell . . .*

After that we often talked and Solete told me this was a
time for contemplation of the departed and I must be alone
with my thoughts. Otherwise I would be overwhelmed. I
was overwhelmed already, I had inadvertently proved his
theory. As he spoke to me I noticed that he had grey-blue

eyes; his general expression was so compassionate that
I could scarcely look, afraid of blurting out some inner
carnage and dissolving entirely. His hands were long and
slender and the skin was so translucent that they looked
blue. I explained that there were occasions, now for example, when the sorrow was so harsh and visceral that I felt as
if I was being disembowelled and this sensation of acute
pain simply made me cry.

'Alas,' he said. 'This condition of mourning becomes
almost constant as you become more established in life and
by the time you reach my age almost everyone you love has
died. For example, it is nearly twenty years since my wife
died, and that is a very long time, and so I mourn and
miss her but somehow I barely remember her. Sometimes
I think I mourn a deceptive memory of her, something I
am clinging onto, salvaged from photographs.'

I said I was so sorry about his wife. But he didn't seem
miserable. He was quiet and composed. His hands were
clasped on his notebook. 'Her name was Asta Rose,' he
said. 'Isn't that a beautiful name?'

I said it was.

'Asta means beloved,' he said. 'She was a professor at the
university, as well, she worked on cosmology and astrophys-
ics.' Solete was a philosopher, he explained. So together
they had encompassed the dying past and the unknown
future. And yet, the stars are the past anyway, I knew that
didn't I? Billions of years old. The past beyond humanity.

'My wife,' said Solete, 'always said that once summoned, life always lives, in some way, in particles, and
the revelations of quantum physics are that we are eternal,
if we only alter the concept of what "we" must mean.'

'It hardly helps with death,' I said. 'Quantum particles. You want the person, not the particles. If they are else-where that's fine but you can't find them. Speak to them.'

'I know,' he said. 'I understand.' And I believed him. He was the only person in the café who didn't make me angry somehow; all that week I had been furious with everyone. Something about his inner peace – without oblivion, or bravado – consoled me, just a little.

Today everything was so ordinary, just the thrum of conver-sation, words drifting through the warm and well-lit room, the clatter of plates, knives scraping. For a long time I was busy, moving food, smiling, accepting tips and saying thank you nicely, and Bevin was looking tense, the worst sort of look for him, any moment he would explode. People started gathering their bags, coats, scarves, I willed them to go.

I was deeply surprised when, at ten p.m., Yorke came in. He moved towards me, as I struggled with a tonne of ill-assorted crockery. I felt embarrassed and exposed and I felt as if he would look down on me, but why? And furthermore, why should I care what he thought?

'There are a few further things I need to, er—' he was saying. Then he noticed that Bevin was glaring at him from the door to the kitchen, looking as if he might come over any moment and scream in his face.

'Who is that man?'

'My boss.'

'When do you finish?'

'In an hour.'

With another glance at Bevin, Anthony ordered a glass of wine. Bevin was busy morphing into an archetype representing Fury but then, it was a cafe, it served wine – what else could he do?

I was meant to be flicking crumbs away with a dishcloth and scouring pans in the kitchen. All sorts of drab and crucial tasks awaited me but still I sidled over with the wine and then I pretended to be clearing things away, putting chairs on tables.

'That boss of yours is a jerk,' said Anthony. 'It's amazing anyone comes back again.' He was reading something leather-bound, purloined from the college library. Crabbed print, mildewed pages.

'Why are you here?'

'Oh, yes,' he said, putting down his book. Stretching his limbs out. 'Well, it's like this. O'Donovan is a career fool. Churchwood too. Of course we all know that.'

'And this is what you came to tell me?'

'No no. I found a letter for you, among Solete's papers.'

He handed me a tightly packed envelope. I took it from him, noticing how his hands always trembled. Intense nerves. Drug addiction? Bevin was wandering round the café in his malign and unnerving way so I started arranging flowers, taking the dead ones out of the vases, putting them in a pile.

'Will the fellows find the book?' I said.

'Petrovka and O'Donovan are at Solete's house at the moment. I don't know what they'll find there.'

'Well, that's reasonable enough,' I said. 'Of course, they'll look in all the obvious places.'

I had to give someone a glass of wine, I had to take away a plate, wipe something, I was darting here and there – Anthony barely noticed – when I got back again he was talking about Pandora's Box – you know, he said, release of forces, good and bad – mostly bad of course – but then other things come out – depends anyway what you regard as anarchic or corrosive – energy – can be bad and good – Blake and the devil, you know –

'Better murder an infant in its cradle – you know that,' he was saying.

'Yes,' I said. I thought I did.

'Still O'Donovan, Petrovka, they're scholars, you know, they're paid not to think.'

A group walked towards the door. Goodbye, I said. I felt as if the night beyond was gulping them down one by one.

'Open your letter,' he said. He leaned towards me, nodding – his eyes shadowed with black circles, that air of anxiety, and now he whispered – 'Really – go to the loo, pretend you're ill – go and read it –don't you want to?'

Now Bevin was behind me, stamping his foot – I was even relieved –

Really – a gentleman had been trying to get my attention for the last five minutes –

Was I expecting to be paid?

A real gentleman, I wondered? With a top hat, with a cane? But no it was just a larded grockle, no top hat, he just wanted to buy a pudding.

Anthony picked up his book. 'Sorry,' he said. 'My fault.'

'Closing now,' said Bevin, just to Anthony, who shrugged irritably. Bevin too. Irritably, Anthony got up. Bevin watched him as he walked across the room, and paused at the door. I assumed it was a commendable effort to annoy Bevin – but then Anthony genuinely seemed to be wavering, as if he was trying to decide whether to turn around again. Then, evidently, he decided to go through –

The door slammed behind him –

By the time I got out of the café everything had finished, the city was closed down. Shivering, I hurried past Pie Hall and the Old Library again, then along the High Street towards the river. Nightingale Hall on the left, its windows blank. A man appeared suddenly, I almost screamed. Oblivious, mist-bound, he faded.

After that I ran up the Cowley Road and all the way to my door. There I fumbled with the key, raged silently. It was that madman Anthony, it was corrosive nerves, I had to calm down –

As soon as I was inside, I slammed the door. Then I opened the letter and before I had even removed my coat or taken off my shoes I began to read:

Jonathan Solete, 29th December 2015

Dear Eliade,

I am sorry I am dead. But you understand the strange bond between the dead and the living and so I wanted to pass this on to you. How did I come to be in this situation? Well, you may ask. Your situation is not mine, I understand. But like me, you were born, however many years ago, and you were at that moment consigned to the realm of time.

Wherever you were beforehand, if anywhere, we do not know. However you are here now, and I was once, before I died, and this is why we can communicate with each other in this way.

At least I hope we can.

I began many years ago, decades and decades, with an idea that I would offer a survey of prevailing theories of reality, with the ultimate aim of offering a helpful guide to reality as a whole, to which the reader might refer, as one might refer to a guide to zebras on a safari tour, for example.

Reality, of course, is a more shifting and peculiar thing than zebras (which also in themselves constitute reality) so my wife Asta and I began with basics and then moved on to more elaborate philosophical and existential conundra. There are many varied theories of reality and they often contradict each other — viz, the religious view of reality contradicts the materialist view of reality, the Cartesian dualistic view contradicts the monist, and so forth. We hoped to chart a course through such stormy dialectics and emerge into the calm waters beyond.

The project was vast. It continues to be vast, and I can no longer even try to complete it. It has failed and yet I am glad.

I have stored my work in a safe place and I suspect you are clear-sighted enough to find it. You will form your own judgements of those around you. I am dead and beyond such concerns. I wish you luck. You have been a great friend of mine. Atque in perpetuum, ave atque vale —

Solete

'Well,' I said to the night. 'Well!'

○ ○ ○

Boomerang
Prophecies

I woke shivering. My dreams had been florid, over-definite, and now I tried to banish them, though the daylight realm was imprinted with residual strangeness. I fumbled for my watch. Five-thirty a.m. I tried to go back to sleep. When I woke for the last time or rather gave up trying to sleep, it was too cold to get out of bed, so I lay for a while, huddled beneath the inadequate eiderdown, then I sneezed continuously for about five minutes, and when that stopped I lay there in a certain amount of consternation and stared around the room. Eventually I went to the window and opened the curtains. Still, the city was drowning in mist, and I could scarcely see the college spires. I went downstairs to the kitchen and called, 'Isabella? Hallo?' My landlady had already gone. There was a pot of lukewarm coffee on the table and some hard-boiled eggs. I was hungry, so I ate eggs and drank coffee, and then I put on my coat and hat and walked out onto the street.

The mist fizzed beneath the lamps. I tried to whistle but the air was so damp, it seemed to muffle my voice. Everyone was moving swiftly, hunched over, perplexed by the cold.

Solete had lived in a college house, on an island called Mesopotamia, between the upper and lower levels of the River Cherwell. It should have been possible to walk there through the grounds of Nightingale Hall. Yet, I lacked sufficient authority in this cloistered university. I was not a member of a college, and therefore, the porter explained, I couldn't enter.

'You need an appointment,' he said, but kindly. Nonetheless I was rebuffed.

I took the longer route, along the side of Nightingale Hall, and through the misty Parkland. It was like twilight out there, like squinting through half-closed eyes. You could look straight at the sun; the mist had doused it entirely. The trees beneath were silhouettes, frozen cobwebs shimmered between the branches. Then, the black shapes of Pie Hall in the distance, a building like an inverted ship. Cold and bleak – I put my face into my scarf. I passed an old chapel, its steeple lost in clouds. I could see the river as it flowed swiftly, curdled by recent rain. The air was full of muffled birdsong. The bridge to Mesopotamia was rickety and glazed with ice, so I slid carefully along, hoping I wouldn't fall into the tumbling waters below.

On the other side of the bridge was a sketchy patch of land, a slight hill, with bricks underneath, but overlaid with moss and grass. Solete's house was built in Oxford stone, those clear white blocks that look so beautiful, contrasted with a deep blue summer sky. Today it was fading into the blankness, like everything else. There were blue shutters, all of them closed. The garden was planted with variegated evergreens, in pale blue, yellow and red. The colours shone beneath the frost.

I was nervous and so I banged too heavily on the door. My head was aching – the cold air, I assumed. I was trying to peer through the window, when a voice made me jump – and the voice knew my name! It said, 'Ah, Eliade. About to break and enter?'

I turned so fast I cricked my neck. For such haste I was rewarded with the smiling smug visage of Dr O'Donovan. I was about to apologise for intruding, I was rubbing my neck and uttering bashful social niceties but he was really too ebullient to care. He even slapped me on the back, as I struggled across a flowerbed.

'You're completely – er – tainted with the outdoors, it's all over you – whatever happened? Look at you!' He pushed a lock of hair from his forehead, so I noticed he was receding fast. In ten years, he would be unrecognisable. Well there was nothing I could do about that! Now he produced a folder from his briefcase, and waved it towards me.

'Is that the *Field Guide*?' I said.

'No!' He was still smiling. 'But it's altogether better than before! We're in luck!'

He was fingering the papers with a rapturous expression, but it all seemed a little staged. As he opened the door, and ushered me inside, he said, 'Well, personally I think they're really very helpful. At times, anyway. Moments of potential help! Stroke of great luck!'

'Moments?'

'Well, you wouldn't want it to be facile, insulting, now would you?'

We were in an art deco hall, full of Indian wicker furniture. The walls were adorned with photographic evidence of Solete's past. Deserts, Alpine mountains, ships, tundra wastelands, photographed in black and white or, later, adventurous incursions into colour. So lete with his wife, Asta, or at times alone. Through warped windows, I could see the snaking silvery river. Everything was age-distorted, dreamlike. The floorboards creaked, the ceilings sloped. The plaster was cracked. I followed O'Donovan into a sitting room. Old ash lay untended in the grate. I crossed to the fireplace and examined the painting. Another river, the Cherwell not the Isis. A female figure was standing on the bank, half-facing the water. Silvery-black hair pulled back to reveal high cheekbones, a strong chin. In line with the sartorial conventions of the time, she was wearing a crinoline and holding a parasol. The sky was white, the branches were skeletal and it seemed intriguing that the painter had chosen to depict her in the natural severity of mid-winter.

The picture was unsigned, and there was a two-word legend, 'At Mesopotamia.'

O'Donovan handed me the folder, took a pipe from his pocket, stuck it into his mouth and struggled to light it. I was about to examine the great revelation but there was a clatter at the door and now Anthony Yorke and Sasha Petrovka emerged into the room. Anthony was looking exhausted and this supplied the perfect contrast to Petrovka, who nodded in a brusque and determined way and went upstairs. 'Know your way around, Sasha?' O'Donovan was shouting as she receded. 'Ah well,' he said, shrugging furiously, then becoming charming again. 'So, a folder. Anthony, a development. Conspicuous.'

'Conspicuous what?' I said.

'What folder?' said Anthony.

O'Donovan smiled and sat down by the empty fireplace, smirking as he fiddled with his pipe. I opened the folder and read the contents. It didn't take long. They were comprised of a list. The list read:

1 — *Boomerang prophecies*
2 — *Happy Clue, hope it relics you fine*
3 — *I am a pig and I like to emanate*
4 — *Monument of Serenity*
5 — *Id It Oh*
6 — *No matter it was nothing*
7 — *Lives in Trivium*

When I looked up, I saw O'Donovan was laughing. He spluttered on his pipe and said, 'Well, you know. They sound like fucking fortune cookies. I told you, he was a trickster. The whole thing, it's just a joke. Cruel. In a way. But we deserve it.'

There was no one to be angry with, except possibly Solete. And he was nowhere. Or elsewhere. O'Donovan was producing a steady stream of apposite remarks, and I noticed that he was wearing an expensive green shirt, a matching handkerchief in his pocket. And then I thought, it was really hardly relevant whether O'Donovan, whoever he was, had a green handkerchief in his pocket. Ruination. Wreckage. Fraud! Anthony was bemused, so I handed him the list and he remained bemused but now his bemusement was laced with anger as well. While Anthony struggled with his emotions I sat on a venerable sofa, and watched the cold river flowing beyond the window. A cushion had spilled feathers everywhere, and I kept finding them in my mouth.

At Mesopotamia

'Well,' said O'Donovan, standing and smoking. 'I'll be off. Nothing else remains. I'm going to the pub.'

'Your charm is incessant,' said Anthony. His hand trembled as he rubbed his forehead. He was leaning for support on the mantelpiece. His body seemed to revert naturally to a hunched position. 'And I don't even believe you. I bet you've been scouring this place for hours.'

'That's fucking slander,' said O'Donovan.

'It's almost certainly the truth,' said Anthony.

'You're a futile tosser. You need to get a grip,' said O'Donovan. With that, he went. I followed him to the door and watched him sauntering away, puffing out smoke. 'O'Donovan! O'Donovan?'

He didn't hear me. Or, he was pretending not to hear me. Either way, he didn't turn round.

Winter trees reflected in the water. It was a strange island, with the cold river flowing onwards, the banks layered with dead reeds. I imagined Solete, dreaming in his garden, a hat over his eyes, his thoughts unknowable now. Besides, our relationship had been cordial, there had been a basic affinity but I had never really understood him deeply, never would – my thoughts were interrupted by a phrase – *boomerang prophecies*!

Why?

Petrovka was still hunting around upstairs; I could hear the floorboards groaning above when I went inside.

'You look tired,' I said to Anthony. He was sitting on the ruined sofa, feathers wafting around him.

'I'm tripping my head off. All this week, I've been having dreams, about something far below . . . ' Shadows under his eyes. Really the man looked out of sorts.

'But we often have such dreams,' I said. 'Burial dreams. Something about the unconscious, so much is half-concealed, the rest.'

'Oh yes, that's all very well, but I was scratching in the dirt.'

'Why?' I said, looking at his fingernails.

He clenched his fists. 'I was in college this morning, trying to remember. I was certain I'd been on the ground. And there was something speaking to me – I don't know where that was coming from.'

'In your dream? You mean?' I said.

'Yes. What else would I mean?'

'You're under strain.'

'Aren't we all?'

'No, not all. Some of us have virtually dispensed with ambition. That reduces the stress levels substantially . . . '

Petrovka came downstairs, looking flushed and disappointed.

'No luck?' said Anthony.

'He was a clever man, Solete, given certain contexts. I mean, if you kept him confined within rubrics.'

'Specific rubrics?' I said.

They paused and looked at me. 'So, he went mad,' said Petrovka. 'He burnt his work. Like Kafka.'

Anthony and Petrovka looked at each other, stalled by mutual ambivalence. Or mutual yearning. I really didn't know.

'Kafka *wanted* to burn his work, or claimed he did, and told Max Brod to effect the order. But Brod refused. And perhaps Kafka knew he would,' said Anthony.

'You mean, he asked him to burn the work, but secretly hoped Brod would fail to execute his request?' I said.

'No no. Kafka issued the order but imagined it not being enacted. And so, Brod proceeded in line with Kafka's imagination, not with the written reality.'

'Christ, he was just old and trashed,' said Petrovka, impatiently. 'Solete, not Kafka. And so, he gave up. He really slumped. Cerebral decay. Come on Anthony, he was raving mad the last few times you saw him.'

'Depends on your definition of mad.'

'He put his toast in his pocket and before he left the table he asked you if you had ever loved the Warden's wife.'

'That's fairly mad,' I said.

'Actually, within the precincts of your average college, it's really not so outlandish,' said Anthony.

With that, Petrovka explained that she had sifted through all the available evidence – notebooks, foolscap, orts, fragments – and there wasn't much else to do. 'He was harmless. I'll come back and try again tomorrow. But I'm not hopeful.'

Anthony looked crushed, briefly. 'Fine,' he said. Gathering himself. 'You go.'

Petrovka nodded at me, nodded at the room, then departed. Through the warped glass we saw her crossing the icy bridge and fading away.

Yorke and I moved from room to room, in silence. The house was gelid, condensation massed on the walls. We went up a spiral staircase to the upper floors, the walls painted white. Battered chandeliers were suspended from the ceiling. Family portraits glared from the walls, and chipped statues posed beneath, semaphoring with stone hands.

'This was Solete's room,' said Anthony, pushing open a door. We moved into a light blue room with a large painting of the English countryside, Romantic style, and a four-poster bed. There was a bay window, overlooking the frosted landscape. I imagined – Solete, sinking onto the bed. His hands weak and clammy. He wanted the old world to consume him but he couldn't focus his mind. Too many worlds and moments. Consoled, always by the fluid view, the light reformed by ancient glass. Reality altered.

'This house belonged to Robert Grosseteste, first Chancellor of the university,' said Anthony. 'He slept in this room. No windows then. Bloody cold.'

No disturbance of the light. Grosseteste shivered, but saw reality clearly. At least, at times.

'Solete bought it when he came back from the war,' said Antony. 'It was completely ruined and he rebuilt it. Expanded it. He lived here for nearly seventy years.'

One morning and then another. He watched the days dawning, one by one. Solete rising, with his wife beside him, or, later, alone. Padding to the door, the floorboards creaking under his feet. The seasons changing beyond the window.

Below, doors opened off a darkened corridor. I opened
one and found a library with dim lighting and oak panel-
ling, a musty smell in the air. I spent a while reading
spines: *Le Morte d'Arthur*, *The Lord of the Rings*, *The House
of the Duchess*, *The Decameron*, *The Princess*, *The Ring and
the Book*. There seemed to be a pattern, I couldn't discern
it. Royalty? Plague? Tale-telling? Anthony waited politely
as I struggled to forge a connection. Then he led me out
of the library and along the corridor again. We walked
through an open kitchen area, plants climbing the walls,
a hearth with copper pots. Another door, and we were in
a long thin dining room, with dull green walls, a trestle
table, curtains swinging in the draught.

Another passage flanked by stone figures, another
doorway, and this next room was white, the shelves full
of Anglo-Saxon poetry. 'Of course, he was the last of his
generation,' said Anthony. 'No one else survived. They
were the war dons, the ones who postponed their careers to
go away and fight. He was seventeen when the war began.
Elegant young men, studying in these sequestered colleges
and then they were blood-stained and terrified, struggling
each day to survive, vomiting with fear and yet concealing
every shudder of dread, every spasm of pure unbridled
horror and they killed so many men, they lost count, and
witnessed the gory death spasms of their comrades and
then, they went back to Oxford. They were supposed
to carry on. As if nothing had happened. At one level,
Petrovka is right. They must all have been latently mad.'

'It wasn't their fault,' I said.

He looked offended. 'I never said it was.'

At the end of a gloomy corridor, there was a pinecone on a tall plinth. The plinth was a metre high, the pinecone just as tall again, immaculately rendered in shiny wood. We both stopped before it. It was the draughty corridor, or the general atmosphere of gloom, but somehow I felt unnerved. The abandoned house, the cold stone, the swift white river beyond. And now, this weird effigy. I stood there for a while, absorbed in the strangeness, trying to understand the object before me.

Masons, Anthony was saying. The pinecone was an ancient symbol of fertility.

'Was Solete a Mason?' I said.

'No. At least, I'm pretty sure he wasn't.'

The pinecone, edifice of Masonic secrecy or fertility symbol, had been carved by Roland Port, of 23 Lake Street, Oxford. There was a little placard, behind the impressive plinth.

'Ah yes, Mr Port,' said Anthony. 'A sculptor of renown.'

'You know him?'

'Not personally. By reputation.'

I wrote down Port's address.

'Did Solete say anything in his letter?' said Anthony.

'He said that he was sorry he was dead. Or rather, when he wrote the letter, he felt he would be sorry, then. Except of course he's dead, so he can't be.'

'Any further clues?'

'No.'

'I think he hated O'Donovan. Wouldn't you?'

Then I saw the time. I had to work. Lunch, I said. 'Christ, I'll be flayed . . .'

'Yes of course,' said Anthony. 'I'll stay here for a while and carry on.'

I said I'd call him later.

'Why?' He shrugged. 'I mean, of course. Yes.' He seemed offended though, that I was going so swiftly. I stood for a moment longer at the Pinecone, waiting perhaps for one last hint.

Nothing!

'Keep your phone on,' I said. 'I'll call you if I have any ideas . . .'

'Most of the time it doesn't work,' he said. 'You know, the mist.'

o o o

The Celestial
Pinecone

Robert Grosseteste, scion of the ancient world, rose to the successive mornings, looked through the open window and saw the river issuing onwards always onwards to the sea. He observed the slow drift of the seasons. The world turning, and time seeming to circle round and round and, yet, his bones creaked in the mornings when he rose and he looked at his hands and realised again, the impossible strange dream – he was old.

Color est lux incorporate perspicuo . . .

Colour is light incorporated in a diaphanous medium. But what is diaphaneity? When is it pure and when is it impure? Grosseteste stares at the broad blue sky slamming onto the summer fields and the gradations of colour, fiery and beautiful, and the sunlight hurts his eyes, and he doesn't know. He believes that the extremes of colour are white, created by such fiery furious light in pure diaphaneity, and black, created by dim light in an impure diaphaneity.

The inflections of sunshine on the water, turning the river blue then gold. Copious or scarce light, bright or dim light, pure or impure diaphaneity. *The sun is in the presence of God*, says Grosseteste. *Its light is the first visible light that shows the species of all colours; and since colour is incorporated light, which due to its incorporation does not move itself to become visible except when an external light is poured onto it, it is clear that colour is born together with visible light . . . Everything which is visible, is so by the nature of light.*

Grosseteste observes – the sunshine boiling across the fields, illuminating the textures of the trees, so they are furry then spiny then florescent, then matted with dark ivy then burnished with gold. *By light we perceive; and we are of the sun. In the beginning there was darkness and no colour at all.* Everything glistens, sparkles and fades. Years pass, and Grosseteste looks at the world beyond and wonders if his eye emits light, or if the world sends light into his eye, and what is all this stuff – this diaphaneity – that swirls between him and all things? That swirls among the objects and creatures of the world, and causes them to be seen?

I walked from Mesopotamia to Nightingale Bridge, with the conversational gurgle of the river beside me. I passed a flock of geese, drifting on the current. At Nightingale Bridge I left the Cherwell and turned to the west, and walked instead along the Isis. On Aristotle Meadow there were students walking swiftly, hunched and forlorn. I moved through mist-glades and dark reaches where the river nearly stalled and then past old drunks rustling home, trying to keep warm, and kids with music in their ears, the endless flow of songs, and an old lady who said, 'It wouldn't be, would it? Would it?' into her phone, as if it really wouldn't be. Could it? At Folly Bridge, there were cars waiting in queues, the steady murmur of the river below. Aristotle Hall stood to the north, with its thunderous bell tolling into the mist. One more hour.

As the bells tolled Roger Bacon conducted his great experiments on Folly Bridge. Magician, shadow-player, and besides, he believed he could control the properties of light and shadow. He watched shapes dance, realised in extremities of colour. Privation and opulence, darkness and brightness. By this, some said, he consorted with the devil.

Bacon, inspired by Grosseteste, by Alhazen and Aristotle, sat in his perishable tower and looked out at the river. He looked at the sun, as it emanated visible power. He believed that every object radiates a force, or a *species*, by which it acts upon other objects. *Fire by its own force dries and consumes and does many things. Therefore, vision must perform the act of seeing by its own force. But the act of seeing is the perception of a visible object at a distance, and therefore vision perceives what is visible by its own force multiplied to the object.*

Moreover, wrote Bacon, *the species of things of the world are not fitted by nature to effect the complete act of vision at once. Hence, these must be aided by the species of the eye, which travels in the locality of the visual pyramid, and changes the medium and ennobles it . . .*

This was not species as Aristotle used the word, to denote his meticulous taxonomies. Bacon meant a form of influence, and he believed that light was particular and extraordinary because it was a visible force, in which influence was apparent. We can see the sunlight issuing from the sun. But we cannot see the wind.

By conducting experiments based on Aristotle's theoretical precepts, he learned not to trust Aristotle.

He fell out of love with theoretical precepts.

He proposed that a balloon of thin copper sheet might be devised and filled with liquid fire; thus it would float in the air as light objects float on water. He used a *camera obscura* to observe eclipses of the Sun.

We know everything through vision, said Bacon, *and perspective is the science of vision by which one understands the structure of the universe.*

If you do not understand *how* you see, you can hardly understand the nature of *what* you see.

Bacon also advised his fellow mortals to protect themselves from malevolent forces, which might destroy them. *Do not be exposed*, said Bacon, *to the rays of dubious planets, and to the inconstant and feminine Moon.*

All afternoon, I worked in the subterranean café, and I thought about how Grosseteste created his taxonomies of light and, therefore, the world. Without light, we are nothing — *In the beginning there was darkness and no colour at all.* Then, the early taxonomies of light. First visible light. Incorporated light. *Everything which is visible, is so by the nature of light.* I spent hours delivering food and thinking that without light, there is no world. No reality — or whatever you call it. However you fashion your phrases, however you refer to the stuff around you. Formlessness. Light and shadow. After a long time, my shift ended, and I walked onto the street. The moon sailed into the sky like a silver balloon – I took care not to become transfixed. *We are of the sun*, Grosseteste wrote. Therefore, we must turn away from the enticing silver moon. But why? Why stand in the sunshine only? Why defame the beautiful and melancholy moon? I thought about Bacon with his countless theories. I had lost the diaphanous realm, or transparency. The mist was opaque. In this turgid realm, far from God and whiteness, I passed defunct factories, converted into flats, sanctified and purged of former traces. The atmosphere was desolate.

Two stone pinecones announced the place: a terraced Victorian cottage, as forlorn as the rest of the street. Roland Port was a small man with sunken eyes and lustrous brown hair. He had known Solete well, he said. He had studied under Solete, long ago, and they had become friends. He was interested, like Solete, in the theory of species of Roger Bacon. But then, said Port, he became more interested in tangible forms, not forces, or species. He concerned himself with material substances. Wood and stone. So, he became a sculptor.

'Of course the irony!' said Port. 'I began to sculpt the most bizarre spiritual symbol in history.'

The pinecone.

'Pinecones,' he said, as we moved along his cluttered hall. The place was decked in variations on this prevailing theme. As a sculptor, he was consistent in subject matter. His creations were mounted on plinths, like Solete's, or were arranged on tables and mantelpieces. His house was small and cramped; its dark rooms filled with Persian rugs, sculptures and pictures. On the walls, as we progressed into his living room, were etchings of the pinecones of history. Port stood beside the evidence.

'You arrive,' he said, 'at the Hall of Justice. Of course, you're dead.'

'Naturally.'

'You have already travelled through the afterlife. The ancient Egyptians were very precise about the details of such a jaunt. Each nobleman, pharaoh, anyone of any remote importance, paid a scribe to portray their journey through the dark reaches of the soul way. The mountainᾱ ous deserts of the afterlife, where you might be threatened by crocodiles, receive guidance from wise baboons and then battle the terrible serpent Apophis until eventually, if you were careful and did not perish, you arrived at the Hall of Justice. There you spoke the names of the gods, you were powerful among them, and eventually the great judge Osiris, the Egyptian fertility god and also the dispenser of Justice stood before you with his scales and weighed your heart. If you failed the test, you were fucked. And that was that – off to be eaten by devils.'

'Devils, not baboons?' I said. Unwisely.

'The baboons are the good guys,' he said. 'The devils eat you. The baboons are sacred and when they bang their chests you bloody well listen. Or you get eaten.'

There was a fire burning in the grate, and the room was fetid. I began to sweat. While I waited for Port to make tea, I examined one of his many pinecone sculptures. This one was about the same size as Solete's, and made of oak, covered with some sort of glaze. It seemed odd to carve a pinecone in oak. Why re⁄render a natural object in a different sort of wood? I stroked it, found it was sticky, then Port returned, bearing a tea set on a silver tray. He shook his head, as if he was surprised and disappointed to find me stroking his Art, then gestured wearily towards a preposterous chaise longue, in mustard yellow. I sat down, apologising. He measured me with a withering glance, as if he often got these sorts of low-grade visitors, who violated protocols. He sat down opposite me, in a Chinese armchair, with wings that extended beyond his head. In general the furniture was too large for his room. And too large for Port himself, so he looked like a small but powerful god, sitting on a throne.

'You came because?' he said.

'Well, the pinecone.'

'And you knew Solete well?'

'Not well. For some reason, he gave me a task.'

'Well, that will be either to torment you or relieve you from other torments he regarded as more significant than whatever torment he had in mind for you.'

'Why would he torment me?'

Port laughed. 'Why the hell not?'

I explained about the book, and how Solete had hidden it, or burnt it, or given it away. How I didn't know. So I was on a quest for something I barely understood, and didn't know if I would recognise when I found it.

'Well, aren't we all?' said Port. He wrinkled up his nose and smiled. He was quite charming, but capricious. So he had an edge to him, as if at any moment he would abruptly cease to be charming. I admired him, for making so many pinecones. Then, I admired him because he somehow resembled a pinecone as well. He had such glossy brown hair. His olive skin gleamed, as if he had been polished. He was a pinecone obsessive, a sociopath, I wondered, then decided that must be unfair. Anyway, why would Solete send me to visit a sociopath?

Still, he was a pinecone fetishist. Why not become obsessed with pollen? Or blossom?

'Why do you make pinecones, and not anything else?' I asked.

'First of all, why anything? Why get up? Why get off that chaise longue? Why not just sink into it forever?'

'Because you would tire of me and ask me to leave?'

'Not even that. You'd tire of your position. You'd leave anyway. And so, we rise into adult life and we fix on an occupation. Or, we get handed one. I didn't like the occupations I was handed. What do you do anyway?'

'I wait on tables.'

'And you do, or do not like it?'

'Sometimes I do, and sometimes I don't.'

'But if you had been given a free choice about what you did, would you have done it?'

'No.'

'Thus, you have been handed something. You wanted something else perhaps, and were not handed it. Perhaps one day you will flip your lid and bugger off, but for now, you go along with it. I was handed something which I didn't want. I was an academic administrator. I discovered that I hated academics. Except Solete. I wanted to be elsewhere, anywhere else, and so I became a sculptor. At first that simply meant I starved, and lived in a dump, in south-east London, with the poor victims of our nation's

apartheid system. But then, I realised that the pinecone is
a form that is imbricate.'

'I've no idea—'

'You must think of it in metaphorical terms, like a fish.
The scales of a fish overlap, don't they? So do the scales
of a pinecone. And thus, these are the classic, Ur-cones.
The central cones of mythical history. They are arranged
in line with the Fibonacci sequence. 1, 1, 2, 3, 5, 8, 13,
21, 34, 55, 89, 144. Divine numbers. The Ancients who
measured and perceived the natural world, and its inherent
occult patterns, were completely transfixed by pinecones.
Wouldn't you be?'

'By fish too?' I said.

'Fish, yes. Christ. Fish. And the feeding of the five
thousand. And the great fish gods of the ancient world.
Poseidon. Neptune. Osiris enjoyed delving into rivers. Fish
everywhere. But we're talking about the Pinecone. And so,
the pinecone.'

Port sat, beating time with his small expressive hands,
and explained to me that the lady pinecone has two sorts
of scale. Fishy-pinescale. Quite beautiful. And the lady
pinecone has the bract scales, which are leaf-like, and the
seed scales which send the elemental issue upon the wind,
to burgeon new life, new numerical sequences. The
further beauty is that the scales are arranged in a spiral –
the ancient iconographic symbol of renewal and fertility. Pinecones open and close to disperse seeds, and for
further functions which are botanical and not symbolical
and less intriguing to us. When the cone has descended
from the tree and lost its attachment to the life-renewing

branch, it continues to open and close, depending on whether the forest floor is damp or dry. Closed, damp. Open, dry.

He opened his hands and closed them to indicate the opening and closing of a pinecone. The sun flickered through the blinds and forged pinecone-shaped shadows on the carpet. Dust drifted, along the beams of light. Roland Port marked a circumference with his hands as if he was spanning the pinecone or the world and then said, 'Cambodia, have you been?'

I shook my head.

'The temple rising from lush jungle below, the sense of primordial grandeur issuing from ancient stone. The major structure of Angkor Wat is the pinecone. But this is hardly surprising, because the major structure of the world in general is the pinecone. Not the earth. The earth is not exactly shaped like a pinecone. It is spherical, but it lacks the Fibonacci overlapping structure. It is a shame that the earth is not precisely a pinecone, as this would explain a great deal. But the world itself is defined and orchestrated by the pinecone, and its buried symbolism lurks within everything. It is associated with fertility, rebirth, sexuality, and also the deepest impulses of the inner eye, spiritual revelation. The integral reality of the Self.'

Now Port hit his stride. He was escalating. The entire room was a pinecone, and he was a pinecone and now he explained to me that reality was a pinecone as well. If you weren't a pinecone, you were essentially not real. I felt myself fading at the edges as he showed me Marduk, the Sumerian god, who was holding a pinecone.

Then, an Assyrian genie, holding a pinecone.

Osiris of the Egyptians, with a pinecone staff, as well as Dionysus of the Greeks.

Lord Shiva, with pinecone hair.

The Freemasons built so many edifices defined by pinecone imagery, that we might become overwhelmed if we tried to represent them all. Port told me that one of his favourite of all the pinecone edifices of Freemasonry is a former Masonic temple in Pennsylvania.

The Nazis, who stole so much from ancient religions, including the Swastika, also appropriated the pinecone.

'The Pope entered London a few years ago,' said Port, 'and people were raging and crying and saluting him on the streets, the usual mania but more importantly, what did he greet them with?'

'A pinecone?' I said.

'Good!'

In his zeal, Port opened a book and showed me – another pinecone. This time, we were in Rome, at the Vatican. A vast stone pinecone, an edifice to another era.

The pinecone was, Port explained, the navel of the world. *Omphalus*. In the original stories, the world emerged from primordial chaos. In the depths of night, a strange sound and a movement and then – the first hill. A protrusion into the nothingness. And that protrusion was the pinecone. Not initially. At first it just looked like a mound, but then, gradually, myth and fable perfected it and it became shaped with celestial scales, the

Fibonacci wonders, and then it became the original force field of life, and then of course it was linked to the human spine and the brain. The spine is the tree of life. The staff. Each one of us has life within us. Creation within us. And at the tip of the staff, at the end of the spine, is the pineal gland. A small endocrine gland, as the contemporary scientists define it, producing melatonin, which affects the circadian rhythms. Sleep and waking, rise and fall. It is shaped like a pinecone. The ancients may not have known this. Or perhaps they did – those embalming lizard men who kept their famous dead so pristine. To enunciate the grave regions of antiquity – and the contemporary formulation of the brain – nearly all vertebrate species have a pineal gland. Yet not the hagfish. And alligators don't have pineal glands and perhaps this is why they are destroyers and indeed hateful. Little eyes. The ancients regarded the pineal gland as the third eye. The sacred all-seeing register of the human being. Of being in general.

'The pineal gland is the only region of the brain that is not divided. It is whole. Integral. And of course you know about Descartes who tried to link the tangible world with the spiritual world, through this tiny gland in the brain. The pineal gland was the seat of the soul, he argued, and therefore where the material and the immaterial might merge and belong, briefly, to each other's remit. This was how Descartes solved his philosophical problems.'

With the pinecone. It was completely logical and no longer surprising. I submitted entirely to the argument. I had no choice. As we sat in the lighted dust of his room, as the sparkling dust settled on pinecones, as the dust was illuminated, Port said that Descartes had enforced the ancient distinctions between the material and the spiritual world, and now we call this Cartesian Dualism. Mind versus body. The church was delighted, and Descartes was spared from censorship, or death. Meanwhile Descartes, who was after all, attempting to be rigorous about his binary division of the universe, realised that if the mind and body were resident in entirely different regions – one physical, one immaterial – then there was no logical way in which they might interrelate. Thus, how could the mind influence the body? How could the mind have dominion over mute matter, and so on? How could the ensuing project of the enlightenment, man as lord of nature, have any meaning at all?

'Perfectly, and beautifully, Descartes crafted a fudge,' said Port. 'A big fat fudge. You understand? You understand what I mean by fudge?'

He was leaning towards me. He was intent on the definition of fudge. His pinecones were glistening in the light, surrounded by swirls of illuminated dust.

'Descartes fudged his philosophy, so he might live. And thus the pineal gland was rendered once more integral. Always integral. This thing of myth and physical embodiment. A thing both physical and immaterial. The little pineal gland, said Descartes, was where the impossible occurred, and the mind communed with the body. Immateriality with materiality. And the church wandered away, nodding its clerical heads and Descartes breathed a sigh of relief. Is not life absurd and beautiful at the same time?'

I had no idea. But it was undeniably true. Whatever it was. While I was trying to work out what the hell he meant, Port showed me another of his sculptures – a bronze hand. It was beautifully rendered. It was lustrous, undeniably elegant and on the thumb there was a pinecone, attached and somehow fused with the hand.

'The pinecone hand is the emblem of the Dionysian, who sees another dimension in madness,' said Port. 'This isn't an original sculpture. I had to copy it myself. The Dionysians of course went into frenzies. In this way, they participated in the divine.'

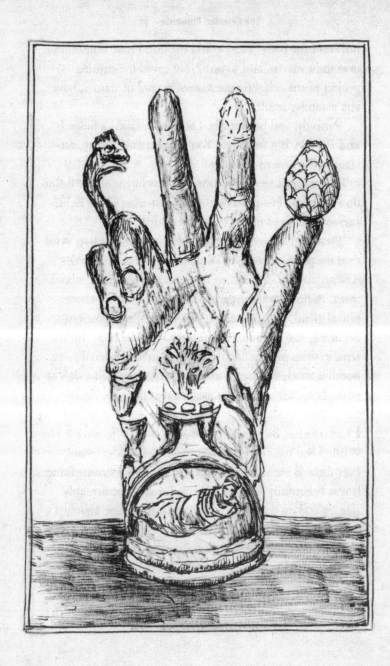

'Was Solete a Dionysian?' I said.

'No,' he said. 'Not many Dionysians about, these days.'

'Why did Solete want a pinecone in his house?' I said, trying again.

'The inner eye sees, but not as our ordinary eyes do. It sees something else. And it fears not the heat of the sun. Or the treachery of the Moon. It is free. It can see what is intrinsic, and it is not distracted by the glittering forms that flicker and confuse the waking eye.'

'Do you have the *Field Guide to Reality*?'

He shook his head. 'Solete would *never* have given me anything important like that. He knows I'm not remotely interested.'

'In reality?'

'Words are terrifying. They are not real. I prefer shapes.'

I didn't know how to answer that. He gazed at me for such a long time I became convinced he had fixed me under a piney thumb. I thought for a moment I might have to ask him to stop, and he was so insistent, with his fixed stare and his conical nature, I became uncomfortable. I felt incredibly hot and my head pounded, at the top of my spine. This was plainly illogical, but it is hard to maintain the tenets of logical deduction when your head is pounding as if it might explode.

'You could try Lydia Cassavetes,' he said, eventually. Now he was urbane again. I felt enervated, as if something was awry. And I was still wondering if Port was, for the time being, sole arbiter of whether things were awry or not. Then I dismissed the thought. Of course he wasn't! He couldn't be! It was just in the pinecone glade, that he was pre-eminent. I had to get out. I felt slightly stifled. It was unfair, he had poured me tea, and told me everything about the pinecone and even now, he was saying –

'She's a bit of a weirdo, but she knew Solete extremely well. She was his greatest friend, after his wife died. We keep strange company in times of crisis.'

He took a pen, and smiled at me. Then, he seemed to be quite harmless. An eccentric sculptor, who spent his life remaking the natural world. Crafting unnatural versions of objects that nature made, effortlessly, spontaneously. It was parody, or a creation fantasy. Or, he liked pinecones. Certainly, that seemed to be undeniable.

He wrote out something, and handed me the piece of paper.

'You'll be lucky if she's there,' he said. 'Or unlucky.'

As he waved me off, he was smiling. I tried to smile back. As I stepped into the torpid ether, my head was still aching. I realised I hadn't eaten for hours. Diaphaneity was elsewhere. The inner eye was closed. Port was blithely issuing me into the further reaches of the unknown.

o o o

UI

Hypatia of Alexandria

I came to Oxford once, when I was fourteen. Before the incident with the Tradescantian Ark and Professor Roberts and Dr Canterbridge. Before the whole thing with the velociraptors. Before that minor stripping of the self I went to Oxford on a day trip, to see the shrine to Shelley the Romantic poet and to venerate antiquity in general. I bowed before the pallid statue, noted the inscription. Then a student in a wound-around scarf asked me if my name was Michelle. It was a joke – I was a parochial fool, he had realised, and so I had gone to the Shelley memorial, simply because I was called Shelley. No matter that in my naïve youth I woke quoting Shelley . . .

I fall upon the thorns of life! I bleed!

And so on. The student made an assumption, and then a joke. It was a great joke, by an anointed wit, and I didn't understand it – lacking wit – until I turned away. Then I hovered on the steps, wondering if I should go back and remonstrate but thinking I would only embarrass myself. So, I went away, with this small stigma attached.

Shelley the poet, and Shelley the unknown imaginary schoolgirl, walked together hand in hand along the river. Then, Shelley threw the schoolgirl in. She bubbled for a while and then like a painting by Millais, she lay on her back and drifted – downstream . . .

Fear not for the future, weep not for the past – Fear not!

I snapped back from – wherever I was – and found my phone was ringing. It was Anthony Yorke and he was saying, 'Nothing. Nothing. At all.'

'Clues?'

'A small statue of a pig.'

'Did it have anything inside it?'

'You mean like a piggy bank? No, it wasn't like that.'

'What was the point of it, then?'

'The point of a statue of a pig? I've no idea.'

When Yorke arrived he was wearing the same ragged suit, inadequate to the prevailing cold, and he looked even more gaunt and pale, as if he were trying to camouflage himself. He was shaking his head.

'We have to walk, before I get hypothermia.'

'Then let's walk.'

We walked with shared determination not to freeze. We turned onto the path along the Isis, winding upstream towards Port Meadow. Beyond, the mist haze and the orange-black sky. Anthony's fingers trembled as he rubbed his forehead. He started telling me about a henge under the Parkland, which had been lost for centuries until it was rediscovered last year. Solete had been greatly interested in the henge because it originally ran past his house.

'Imagine it; running all round the Parkland, they think . . .' he said, waving his arms. 'Don't you see? Solete's house, it's just on the eastern edge. And then Nightingale Hall is just slightly further along, to the south-east. Aristotle Hall is at the southern tip. Pie Hall, the western edge. Solete walked around it every day. He existed in the henge – woke and slept and worked. Me too, that's why he's dragged me in.'

'I really don't think the henge has anything to do with it,' I said.

'Well what do you know? You've spent the afternoon discussing pinecones.'

'With a man who actually resembled a pinecone.'

'Well, that's even more ludicrous.'

Anthony was moving hastily away. 'You're moving too slowly,' he said, over his shoulder. 'My wardrobe is calculated on the basis that I move swiftly, all day. If I slow down, I die pretty immediately.'

The city was adrift in mist and when you reached the outskirts, when you slunk beyond the streets and lost the punctuations of lamps and cars and people, there was just this dim slur of land, with coils of mist above it, around it. Engulfing you as you tried to cross it. There was a general hum emanating from somewhere. Occasional rustling in the hedgerows, and, from the river, the sudden splash of an animal diving in.

'Transparency is an aspiration,' I said. 'But wouldn't it be strange, if you could see things clearly? I mean, all things?'

Anthony didn't reply. He was too busy trying not to freeze.

The shadows lengthened. The mist turned silver. We turned to the west, into the realm of the dying sun. The trees whispered above, and I was thinking how long-gone people had walked the banks of the Isis, and vanished, one by one. We were on Port Meadow, heading north, and

now I heard the sound of singing. Mournful, soft, drifting
on the currents of mist. I wondered, anyway, why I was
pursuing this trail of debris. Pinecones and the inner eye.
I am a pig and I like to emanate. A sacrifice? A pineal pig?
Then I was furious with myself. I thought – you don't have
to believe that man Port, with his house cluttered with
unnatural objects! I saw a bird, darting above the treetops,
darting out of the creeping shadows of the forest into silent
spaces of cloud and mist. The bridge creaked as we passed
over it and then I heard the song –

> *Millions of years is the name*
> *Green lake is the name of the other a pool of cool liquid*
> *Otherwise said millions of years is the name*

I had no idea what that meant. For a moment I wasn't even
entirely sure where I was, but then I saw Anthony hurrying along ahead of me, and that recalled me to the present.
I saw a boat, moored under a bridge, and now I could just
discern the name on the bow: *HYPATIA.*

'More scraps,' said Anthony, dolefully. 'I bet she's mad.'

'In what sense of the word?'

'Oh don't start. She'll be a raving mad hippy with wild
staring eyes. She'll offer you a joint and you'll start raving
about pigs, until we have to go home.'

'Sounds like a delightful evening.'

We stood at the edge of the boat, looking at the neat
word: *HYPATIA.* Someone who could paint so neatly
couldn't be raving mad.

Surely?

Now the voice intoned again –

Millions of years is the name
Green lake is the name of the other
A pool of cool liquid, otherwise said
Millions of years is the name of the one
Green lake is the name of the other . . .

I knocked. The singing stopped.
There was a pause.

The cabin door opened, abruptly. A woman appeared.
She was a beautiful thin hippy with long black hair. She
didn't have wild staring eyes at all. She had considered
and quite frightening eyes, and she turned them on me so
I was flamed by the fiery force of her gaze, as she looked us
up and down. Then I waited for her to open her elegant
mouth and say Begone! Strangers! Fade into the ethereal
night! While we all waited, Anthony started shivering
violently.

'He has to move, or he dies,' I said.

'Tell him to move, then. Away from my boat. And
off to where he wants to go,' said the hippy who must be
Cassavetes.

'The song was very nice,' I said.

'I'm busy,' she said. 'Entirely. What's your problem?
Did someone tell you to come?'

'Roland Port.'

'What does that freaky Ptolemite want with me? Tell
him to get off back to his pinecones.'

'I did the whole pinecone thing with him, in fact, but
when the pinecones were all done, and we had traversed the
whole of history via the pinecone he still couldn't help me.'

Anthony was stamping his feet, puffing on his hands and doing a remarkable impression of a man who was about to succumb to the elements.

'What do you need help with?' said Cassavetes. At this point she was not exactly friendly, but it seemed she was other than overtly hostile. This was a beginning. It was an improvement.

Therefore, I explained that Solete had given me a task. It was ironic, I said. And now Port. His house of many cones. He had sent me over to her. It was a long walk in the mist. Everything was so indeterminate. Anthony kept complaining about the weather. This thick gelid air, it got into your lungs, so you thought you might choke on the cold. Really we just wondered if she had the book.

'Which book?'

'It might be called *A Field Guide to Reality*. Or it might be called something else. But it was by Solete. We think. We hope anyway.'

At that, she shook her head. 'Absolutely not.'

'You don't?' said Anthony, hurtling into the conversa-tion. 'Or you don't want to tell us?'

'I don't have it, and I wouldn't give it to you, even if I did,' she said.

'Fucking fine. Let's go.' Anthony started to trudge away, head down. I was about to go after him when the hippy relented.

'Oh come in,' said Cassavetes. 'Just come down into the boat. You ridiculous parody of a faint-hearted academic and you – you, who keeps talking about pinecones. Just come into the boat. I was just making some food. Solete was a great old friend of mine. I've been ill since he died. One of the last people I liked.'

Yorke shrugged off her insult, and stumbled onto the boat. He seemed not to care who she was, so long as he was warm. As he went down the companionway he started sneezing violently. 'Christ, do be quiet,' said Cassavates. But when we entered the cabin she threw him a blanket. He huddled into it, sitting on a low bunk, rubbing his nose.

An oil lamp was swinging above our heads. The place was rammed with books and detritus. If books are detritus too, then the place was simply rammed with detritus. Every surface, every region, was full of papers, books, pencils, drawings of the river, tastefully executed, musical instruments, compasses, maps, pot plants, plates, cups, teapots. A cat mewed from below; Cassavetes leaned down and stroked it. There was a pan steaming on the stove, and Cassavates dished out bean stew. We ate on tin plates.

Cassavetes was wearing black leggings, and thick socks, and a long, floral dress which swirled about as she moved. Her long dark hair was held in place with a floral scarf. She looked like a younger version of the woman in Solete's painting. Except that woman had been tenuous and pensive, and Cassavetes was firm and unyielding. She spoke with great conviction. She made slightly intimidating eye contact. Anthony faded into his blanket. Occasionally he sneezed. So she turned her gaze onto me.

She rustled through the papers and found a photograph of Solete. He was young, tall and blond, standing with his arm around Asta Rose, who I recognised from the photos in his room. He was wearing a white suit, a boater with a striped ribbon.

'He looks happy,' I said.

'He was an exceptionally happy man. Didn't you find?'

'Yes, I did. Or, at least, stoical.'

'No, no he wasn't a stoic. Foolish materialist fools. Don't you think? All is lost, we're done for, best put a brave face on it. Fools!'

'What, you mean, you've got the answer?' said Yorke, in a distant voice. I looked across at him. He had stopped shivering but he looked deeply white. 'Do pass it on,' he said. Still struggling.

'My father was an academic,' said Cassavetes, ignoring Anthony. 'He was hugely involved with Egyptian archaeology. Spent his life digging in sand. Stuck to his fingers. Said it got in his lungs. He hated it. Coughed out sand, even when he came home. Vomited sand. Anyway, my father as you can imagine really hated sand, but he always went back, dug away again. Found minuscule relics.'

'Relics again,' said Anthony.

'Yes, but you can find a relic and understand nothing about the society,' said Cassavetes. 'The relic is just a thing – and then – you invent, often. My father got in terrible trouble for inventing. But I stood by him. It turned out he hadn't invented anything. Everyone else, all the stoics, had just got it all wrong. They were so concerned with their own funny worldview, they couldn't fathom the minds of the Ancient Egyptians. You can get trapped, can't you? Funny, isn't it? Tragic for my father but laced with irony. Did you know Solete well?'

'Not really,' I said.

'What about you, shivering man?' she said, to Anthony. 'Why are you here?'

'You tell me,' said Anthony. 'I walk from scrap to scrap.
I am cold.'

'Perhaps you are a clue,' said Cassavetes.

'Why is your boat called Hypatia?' said Anthony.

Cassavetes leaned back and paused. The hurricane
lantern swayed again, so her face became a mask, theatrical
shadows around her eyes. And thus, we arrived into Cassavetes's theory of everything — as told through the story of
Hypatia. Like Port, she had a prevailing theme. Anthony
was still rubbing his arms and shivering, but now he settled
down, reclining against the wall, as if he was glad he didn't
have to venture outside. As Cassavetes spoke she moved her
fingers, and the candlelight projected them across the walls,
so they were magnified and animated, like a lantern show.

Hypatia was a consummate genius, Cassavetes explained.
History was generally mistaken about anything that mat-
tered, and this was why Hypatia languished mainly in
obscurity. Born sometime between 350–370 AD, she was
tutored by her brilliant father, Theon, who recognised the
talents of his daughter. Theon had a post at the museum
in Alexandria, where he taught mathematics, physics and
astronomy. Through her father, Hypatia became familiar
with the works of Plotinus, Aristotle and Plato, as well
as with Euclidian geometry.

Hypatia imagined the starry expanse wherein reside
the forces of the universe, interior virtues. In line with
the teachings of Plato and Plotinus, she believed that
there is an ultimate reality, beyond the reach of thought or
language. In life, we may aim towards this ultimate reality,

yet we can never fully grasp it and it can never be precisely described.

Hypatia was staggeringly beautiful, but she also took drastic measures to disperse the effects of her beauty on her students. To one mystified acolyte, she revealed her soiled undergarments, and explained, on this basis, the fleeting and insufficient nature of the physical realm.

Hypatia, in her study, in a room overlooking the sea. A few centuries later Alhazen will be in Cairo, imbibing the dust that blows in from the desert, and pondering the nature of perception. Hypatia is less moved by dust, but particles and integers fill her with awe. She believes you might relay the mysteries of the universe in numbers. And yet, this is not invention, she claims; it is an acknowledgement of the eternal realities. Numbers are inherent to the mystery around her. The mysteries are mathematical and numbers recur throughout nature – in the repetitions of the planet, as it turns in space, and in the repetitions of the diurnal round, twenty-four hours, light and darkness. Referring back to Ancient Babylonians, Sumerians, long lost tribes again, Hypatia understands that there are twelve hours in the day, twelve hours in the night, and, with reference to the later work of Ptolemy, sixty minutes in an hour, sixty seconds in a minute. Her finite life is composed of increments.

As a neoPlatonist, Hypatia attracts the suspicion of the Christian authorities. In 412 AD, Cyril becomes patriarch of Alexandria. The Roman prefect there is Orestes, a friend of Hypatia. Cyril wants to assert the power of the church; Orestes seeks to defend the boundaries of the state.

Their feud has become increasingly acrimonious. Hypatia's friendship with Orestes, combined with her supposedly pagan views, and her refusal to supplant the realm of Platonic forms for the Christian realm of the spirit, makes her a focal point for the unrest. There are struggles between Christians and non-Christians. In one such riot, Hypatia is attacked by a mob of Christians who jeer at her, call her a pagan. She is torn from her chariot, stripped naked, dragged to the church. Her flesh is scraped from her bones with oyster shells, and her quivering limbs are delivered to the flames.

Cyril, who worked so hard to incite the hordes to this act of psychotic murder, is later canonised by a grateful church.

In 391 AD, the library at Alexandria was burnt to the ground, by another crowd of fanatic monks, under orders from Archbishop Theophilus. In 529 AD, Plato's Academy was closed by Justinian. Such Platonic lines of enquiry were no longer approved. Thought must be constrained by truth, of course.

Nearly a millennium later, we might imagine Raphael finishing his *School of Athens* fresco. Perhaps a few esteemed church elders arrive to view this work, to ensure that it is sufficiently pious. One particularly devout and worshipful bishop asks Raphael why he has placed a woman between Heraclitus and Diogenes. This must be a mistake, says the bishop. A woman! Raphael explains that the offending woman is Hypatia, the most famous student of the School of Athens. Naturally, the good bishop insists that this aberrant female is immediately removed. *Knowledge of her runs counter to the belief of the faithful! Otherwise the picture is acceptable.*

Thus are rectitude and propriety maintained, throughout history, by our anointed sages.

'So that was the story of Hypatia and why I named my boat after her,' Cassavetes was saying. 'After her and all the other wise women burnt at the stake because they were assumed to be wrong and evil, by those who were wrong and evil themselves. And that's why when people knock on my door in the dwindling dusk, with the cold winds blasting in from the north I tell them to go away. Unless they have good reason to come and see me.'

'Did we have good reason?' I said.

'You were friends of Solete. And that man has no spine for the cold.' She turned to Anthony, who was still huddled in the shadows. From the shadows, he nodded. 'I'm much better now,' he said. 'Though naturally very sorry about Hypatia. Terrible scene.'

I looked at her store of books. Plotinus. Plato. Hypatia, of course. *De Colore* by Grosseteste.

'Do you move your boat along the river?' Anthony was saying.

'Rarely,' said Cassavetes. 'This is an old town, but I like the way it whines and hums. Too much silence makes my head ache.'

'O'Donovan says it's all just a joke,' said Anthony. 'The *Field Guide to Reality*. A paradox.'

'Well, O'Donovan, whoever he is, could be right. Or

wrong. He sounds as if he's likely to be wrong. Enunciators are generally wrong.'

'An enunciator being?'

'A person who enunciates. Idiots, in general.'

'But, haven't we been – enunciating? Just now?' said
Anthony.

'Depends on the way you do it, as with everything. You
should go to the mechanical magicians. Solete liked to visit
them. The worst offenders. Here . . . '

Like Roland Port before her, Cassavetes wrote down
something on a piece of paper. Another scrap. She handed
it to me, though Yorke put out his hand. When I read it in
the flickering candlelight it said:

> *Benighted men of little meaning.*
> *The mechanical magicians are at 32 Swinbrook Lane*

'But don't go too far,' she said.

Yes, right, I almost said. Absolutely. Not too far.

'But will they actually help?' said Anthony.

'What do you mean by help?'

That was impossible to answer. So we all went up onto
the bank, and I thanked Cassavetes, while Anthony murmured along. Because it was so dark and drear, she offered
us a lantern. 'You can return it to me later this week,' she
said. 'I'll be around.'

I thanked her and took the lantern, promising to bring it
back. I could see Anthony was starting to shiver again.

'Why did Solete associate with the mechanical magicians?' I said. 'If you think they are such fools?'

'The fool thinks he is wise, the wise man knows he's a
fool,' said Cassavetes. 'Then you have the wise man, who

knows he is a fool, and therefore occasionally gets confused and consorts with genuine fools who are infinitely more foolish than he is — because of course he is not a fool but a wise man, after all.'

I didn't really know how to respond.

'It's a category error,' said Cassavetes.

The wind hissed along the banks, and Yorke was hurrying along, so I had to hurry as well just to stay beside him. The moon was beautiful and injurious, I had been told. The moon invoked a shadow religion, the old religion of the pagans, who were snuffed out by marauding tribes with their new censorious gods. Hypatia deferred to shadows from the Platonic era, and then she was condemned, and hurled into the flames.

A boat moved slowly along, its stern lights casting a faint reddish glow on the water. It retreated upstream, towards the west. Beyond the meadow, the city hummed, referring a background glow of orange light into the ether. The mist swirled above, dispersing and accumulating again. We moved onto a dry, frosted path, towards the bridge into Jericho.

'He only wants to infect you with his preoccupations,' said Anthony. 'Like a contagious invalid. A plague carrier,' he added.

'Why say that?'

'Solete was jolted by the immense indifference of the skies, the shocking realisation of the limitations to our lives. It had all been fine for generations. Not fine, of course, people lived and died and lost those they loved, and their babies died in droves and they mourned, they spent their lives in a state of perpetual mourning. And death was not in the background, something you try to ignore, it was prevalent, all the time. But they had a kind of faith, in something else, a consolatory elsewhere, and perhaps that helped. Then something changed the human imagination, and celestial wraiths were banished and Solete fell into the abyss, that's all.'

'You mean, he suffered from a general crisis of faith?'

'Undoubtedly. He wanted certainty. Couldn't find it. So decided to drag everyone else in. Piss them off as well.'

A train hammered along the tracks, causing flocks of birds to issue from the silhouetted trees. Mist curdling across the white lake. Millions of years.

In the darkness, we became conspiratorial. Yorke told me that when he was a child he played a game. With his brother, Robert, he imagined – in the dreamscape of childhood, in which fantasy and reality are elided – that the river beyond his house – the Avon, outside Bristol – had powers to reincarnate the dead. One day, they took a dead mouse and threw it into the water. They went back the following day to await the return. Sometimes the animals did not reveal themselves, and thus, you might say with cold logic, could not be said categorically to have returned, but like scientists and practitioners through the ages this failed to deter Anthony and his brother. They simply imagined that the animals had returned elsewhere, to some other point, and they prepared themselves for the next experiment. They threw another animal into the water, and returned the following day. Anthony couldn't remember why they always waited twenty-four hours, or how precise the elapse was. He remembered the animals returned at sunset. Symbolically this was quite illogical; you might expect them to return instead, if it were even feasible that they might return at all, at dawn, a new beginning, and so on. But quibbling about the relative plausibility of elements within an implausible scenario seems futile. Anthony and his brother dallied with their improbable experiments in reincarnation for some years and then, their mother died, and of course they realised, the dead don't return, the loss is complete. And you can sit and chant by the river, and if this consoles you then that's fine, but it does nothing to change the bewildering permutations of reality around you.

'I'm very sorry about your mother,' I said. He received the obligatory phrase.

'No one ever gets over the death of a parent,' he said. 'But you carry on. You are even happy, often, and you realise this is what your beloved parent would have wanted. They didn't want you to spend the rest of your life bereft and forlorn. They birthed you and hoped that you might be happy despite mortal asperities and despite any further vicissitudes that might be reserved particularly for you. It is of course completely usual.'

'But you were children.' I had been sufficiently demolished by the death of my father, and I was an autonomous adult, who had lived apart from him for years. But to lose a parent, when you were dependent, and you saw them every day, and then suddenly – nothing! The completeness of the loss must be far more shocking, I thought. I was trying to say something like that, but he interjected. He sounded impatient.

'Time has a way of blurring the distinctions between young and old. In the past, long ago, my mother disappeared.'

'What happened to your brother?'

'He became accounts manager for a family-owned stationery firm in Norbiton,' said Anthony. 'He has four kids. He's mainly happy.'

'I lost my father too,' I said. 'A couple of years ago.'

'You didn't lose him, that's an erroneous cliché.'

I hadn't expected the usual platitudes. Not from this shuffling wind-chilled man. But, I had perhaps expected – some vague expression of remorse.

'It's a convention, obviously,' I said, rebuffed. 'Why be awkward?'

'I just meant, it wasn't your fault. You didn't mislay him, by carelessness. Did you?'

'It's an expression!' I was abruptly furious. There were many possible causes of my fury – the vagaries of mist, the equal or perhaps even greater indeterminacy of existence and then Yorke's foolish precision with language, which seemed ludicrous, especially in the circumstances! Especially in response to something as insane as death!

'Get a coat, for a start,' I said. 'And don't talk to me about grammatical precision again. You're a scholar. You're a professional fraudster.'

'I am not,' he said. He was looking across at me. Perhaps he had even slowed down, to register my fury.

'You're effectively a liar. A fantasist!'

That produced a pause. For a while we walked inside the pause, which spread as the darkness spread across the meadow. Animals punctuated the silence, as if they were trying to help – a last flurry of birdsong and unknown beasts rustling through the hedgerows. All nature chorused and then, suddenly, fell silent. The pause swept across the darkened fields.

Yorke was hastening along again, shuddering and occasionally stumbling on the hard ground.

The treacherous moon rose above the houses, filling the mist with injurious light.

On the streets, other people moved along. Bustling, with temerity. 'Got to get to the fucking you know,' said one man to another as they hastened past.

'It just isn't right. That tumbling gait.'

'Pagans.'

The mist, smudging every sound I heard. I blamed the elements then I blamed my own hyperactive imagination. The two men were absorbed into the prevailing whiteness. The pause by now was such a leviathan that it squatted above the houses and threatened even to drink the mist.

'Are you offended?' I said, eventually. Even though I was offended first.

'Not remotely,' said Anthony, sounding offended. 'Why would I be offended?'

He walked away, into the mist.

That night I shivered in my bed, and heard cars sliding down the smothered street, and neighbours creaking inside their houses. I drifted in and out of sleep. I was angry about the conversation with Yorke. Then I thought it was a way of transferring other causes of irritation, and really his words had been nothing. He had been trying to tell me – it wasn't my fault. Just as it wasn't his fault. It wasn't anyone's fault.

Everyone was blameless, he had meant to say. He just phrased it badly.

I was soothing myself with this reinterpretation, and concluding that this was quite right, and tomorrow I would apologise for misunderstanding him, but how would I do that, I thought? I wasn't even allowed into the college, that hallowed sanctuary! So that made me angry again. And I wondered why he was hanging around anyway? With his bizarre dress code and his frankly rigid views on the proper use of language . . . ? Why?

While I was musing on that question, I fell asleep . . .

So I dreamed I was standing in a room, in front of a fire. Sparks leapt like fireflies, smoke streamed upwards to the sky.

I was with Solete, in his house, as he gathered his notes, burnt them in the fireplace. I could smell the ash, I warmed my hands on the flames. When the fire had died, and the last scraps were piles of grey ash, I heard the water lapping the shore, and the soft sound of voices. The door to the bedroom was forced open, and the wind was full of dust. And Solete sank to the floor, curling his arms above his head.

He felt himself being lifted by two sets of hands. He felt a splash of water on his ankles, and then he was in a boat. Two men were smoking quietly, their faces obscured, speaking a language he didn't understand. They rowed him slowly downstream, and he saw the fluted ornaments,

and smelt the sickly dew of perfume. The pale moon above him.

For a moment it was so beautiful that in my dream, I wept.

○ ○ ○

VII

The Mechanical
Magicians

Now, when I woke to the residual blankness of the sky, I had to make an effort to summon myself, and then to determine what was real and what was not. I was definitely not Solete, that was clear. I was not standing in his room and watching him being – carried away. I was not on the wind-lashed meadow, listening to the pained cries of waterfowl. Instead, voices gurgled through the wall, and my landlady was rummaging briskly in the corridor, slamming doors. I moved to the window and looked out but that didn't clarify much. The street was mist-laden and once more predominantly white. Cars moved into further regions of whiteness.

I found my watch and succumbed to ritual haste.

In the café the hordes were ill-tempered. I ran around distributing food – to people who worked in the museum, who bickered in the lecture halls, and the students with their scowls and scarves – I ladled beans onto plates, handed them to random people, as they brayed back at me –

'More beans please . . . Call that a portion of chips? I don't like milk, no milk for me . . . No bloody milk, were you not listening? Have you become inattentive? How could you?'

How could I?

Again, I was late. Subliminal reluctance. Hardly even subliminal. Reluctance ingrained into my being. There were things I wanted to say back to these vociferous hordes, but I wasn't sure they really wanted to hear them.

Well, sir – perception is a prevailing mystery of thought.
I didn't think that would go down well at all.

Instead I said: 'Shall I write up the specials on the
board?' I made sure the bottles were in the fridge and all
turned the same way, labels showing, I put more coffee in
the coffee machine, I poured out coffee for some hoary old
gentleman in loafers . . .

Who said, 'Thank you dear' as I said, 'Thank you sir.'
I took the money from his hoary old fingers, opened up the
till, gave him his change . . .

Clink clink go the coffee spoons, and there's the whir-
ring of some industrial cleaning device in the kitchen, and
the cook rages through the hatch, 'Get the stuff out now.
It's going cold!' Then the illustrious denizens of Oxford
really will revolt . . . Smash the place, storm the kitchen,
massacre the chefs . . .

Chips sir? Beans sir? Fried egg or poached madam? Did
you know I had a dream last night? I was Solete, or was I
standing beside him? I'm not entirely sure . . . And suddenly – in my dream, I think – I was here, in this café once
again, dishing out baked beans, chips, asking you if you
want ketchup or any other sauces – madam, I really think
you were there too – I'm sure of it – your irritable gaze
and this silk thing you've wound around your neck – that
too – and we were just discussing whether you wanted
the burger or the chicken, and whether the chicken had
been cooked today – yes, even in this transcendental ghost
zone, you were particular about the freshness of your meat,
I remember it so well – and then – well! There was a
whooshing sound – a strange, disturbing whoosh and

then suddenly – whoosh – you vanished! Sorry to say, you were first to go! And then – carnage – everything got smashed and fell apart, the whole edifice crumbled, cracked was the roof, shattered were the windows, and I –

Well, I have to confess, then I woke up . . . And now I'm here!

I kept looking at the door, and I wondered if I was expecting Solete, or Yorke. Somehow I felt nervous, as if someone might soon appear. I kept getting distracted, and then, suddenly, I was recalled, by a reasonable request from a customer or, increasingly, a complaint.

Ah yes, bread and butter, of course, there's an extra charge, fifty pence, is that alright . . . Oh alright, no I understand entirely . . . Yes I'm so sorry you feel that's exorbitant . . .

I'm just so so sorry.

Good luck . . . Farewell . . .

It ran on, and on . . . I tried to remember the categories of separation. On one hand, my dreams, the fantastical bedlam of unconscious thought. On the other, the material aspects of the waking day. In this tangible present, I had to attend to – for example – the woman pitching in with a committed complaint about her burger. She was very upset about some aspect of this thing, so I said, 'Yes, of course, I'm so sorry, let me take that for you . . . ' Then there was the man who couldn't get down the steps – so off I went, apologising profusely, dreadful indeed . . .

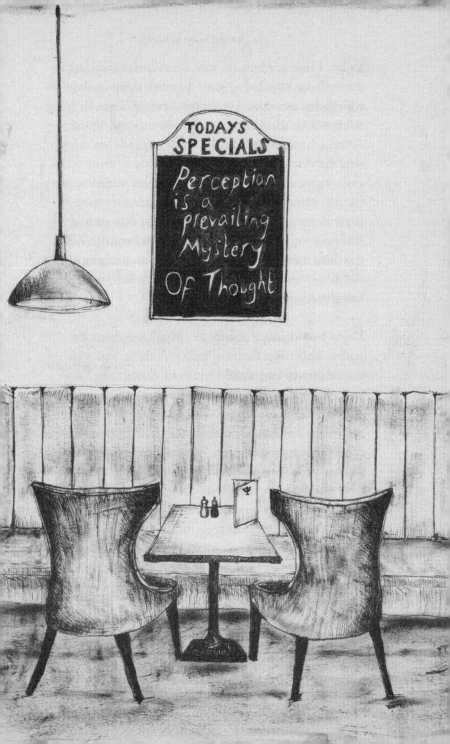

When I emerged from the café, the mist was sparkling in the sunlight. I walked towards the north along roads lined with gothic mansions. For a while I cursed Yorke for being so capricious. How was I meant to understand him? Even this single individual was obscure to me, and then there were the shadowy legions of the dead, and so many traces, clues, signs, all these moments when reality seemed to jump – and to where? From where? I had Cassavetes's scrap of paper in my gloved hand. *Benighted men of little meaning. The mechanical magicians . . .* That was hardly reassuring! What was 'little meaning?' Was it better than 'no meaning at all?' But worse than 'masses of meaning'? Why were they benighted, anyway?

Buses hammering alongside me. Cyclists dodging the traffic. There were the usual gargoyles above, and ornamental turrets, high arched windows. Swinbrook Lane was a semi-bucolic enclave, built for long-vanished dons. Now it was full of oligarchs and celebrities who had run away from London. Or perhaps they lived in London too, came here for the weekends. Anything was possible when you had a Range Rover with the number plate **SOV 13T**. That made things pretty clear. There was a walled garden, full of spiny yuccas and rhododendrons. Robins perched on fragile branches, blackbirds trilling far above. Aside from this, the mechanical magicians were somehow still resident in a white Georgian mansion, an anomaly among redbrick temples. There was an imperious gate with a buzzer. I was told by a melancholy voice to wait, and someone would come to let me in. After a long time, a man walked towards me. He was swaddled in scarves, and limping noticeably. When we shook hands he told me he was called Richard Mortimer, and he was very sorry to hear that Solete was no longer with us. A fine euphemism! The professor had been a distinguished associate of the museum and so now Mortimer wondered if I would like a tour?

We went through a marble hall, littered with busts of the eminent, in creepy white marble. Then we ascended in a silver lift. Meanwhile Mortimer rustled in his smart suit, and tugged his ear. He was like an uncertain, overgrown child. But then, aren't we all, in truth?

At the next floor, the lift stopped, the door opened.

'We keep an archive,' said Mortimer. 'It's a museum of past theories. Scientific theories rise and fall. Like people. The thing is to accumulate evidence. Wouldn't you say?'

'Did Solete come here a lot?'

'He was a frequent and welcome guest.'

The museum was layered into eras of history, and epochs of thought, and then there were further categories within the layers. Mortimer toured me for a while through vast rooms filled with significant objects. We stood beside glass cases, looking at the exhibits.

(**1**) A jug, a pot, a shattered plinth. A boat of small proportions, decayed. A knife, a spoon, some broken bowls. Coins of many eras, heads of emperors and kings and queens, ragged edges, tarnished. Innumerable shards, fragments, ceramic scraps, glassware, old green bottles –

A casket, clasps decayed, empty when opened –
Animal bones, disordered, midden-waste –

(**b**) Photograph: the remnants of many graves, disordered.

(**c**) Foundations of a wood henge, running in a circle with the circumference incorporating the banks of the river, Mesopotamia, Pie Hall, Nightingale Hall – photographic evidence – wooden foundations decayed.

(**d**) Relics too lichen-stained and degraded for salvation, almost indistinguishable from the surrounding earth.

(**e**) A stick, inserted into the ground, wherein a shadow was apprehended by the Ancient Egyptians and thereby the curvature of the planet.

(**f**) A sundial from the Ancient Egyptians, wherein the regions of daylight were divided into twelve hours, unequal in length depending on the season.

(**g**) Mathematical instruments from which the great Ptolemy in *The Almagest* was able to divide the globe into increments.

(**h**) The first mechanical clock indicating fixed minutes.

We walked through one echoing room and another, and through these serried regions of the past. Steadily, the soft voice of Richard Mortimer urged me along. He was telling me about the earliest scientific experiments in Oxford,

and how Grosseteste was one of the pioneers of experimental rather than purely conceptual process, along with
Roger Bacon thereafter, and of course this radically altered
what you placed in your museum. You were no longer
confined to the purely theoretical, as Aristotle was, for
example. You had tangible proof of your theories. These
theories changed all the time, which made it a nightmare
for a curator.

I made noises expressing deep sympathy.

This was a museum of answered questions, and questions that had never been answered but had eventually
been castigated as the wrong questions, and abandoned.
Unanswered.

And also, answers that had turned out to be the wrong
answers to the right questions.

First, humans imagined the sun circling the fixed earth,
and all the stars moving across the night sky. Then reality changed, they changed, and they imagined the earth
moving around the sun. And all the stars in orbit, and
everything became a great moving circulating force field
of universal matter and within this force field were great
patches which were gaps –

They called these gaps the Ether –

And the Ether was Real.

Until it was abandoned and became unreal, and was
never mentioned again, except by poets and lunatics.

And so, the Ether became something else, and was
named – Dark Matter, and Dark Energy. Still no one
knew precisely what it was, but they assumed it was not

Ether, and had other qualities suggested by these other names.

Then the theories changed again, and again.

The universe as a series of triangles.

The universe defined by hypothetical one-dimensional subatomic particles having the dynamic properties of a flexible loop, called cosmic string.

The universe expanding.

The universe contracting.

The universe as infinite.

The universe as finite.

Time as linear and constant throughout the ages.

Time as relative.

Light emanating from the eye, and illuminating the objects we apprehend.

The objects emanating light into the eye.

Everything being illuminated by the eye. Or, reality as luminous, the eye as the passive recipient of such luminosity.

Darkness as the perpetual state of everything.

The great ages of reality, represented in the stars. Cumulative light, from the long distant past. Background radiation from the origins of time.

This was a museum of madmen who had been condemned and castigated and even executed on the grounds of heresy and madness, and later been revered and commemorated.

Theoreticians, alchemists, physicists, cartographers, genius
women who were duly murdered –

(**i**) Roger Bacon, running through the hostile crowds,
dreaming of shadows and of flying machines. Baiting
his contemporaries until they denounced him.

(**j**) William of Ockham, harried by almost everyone.

(**k**) Galileo, condemned by the inquisition. This man
devised an apparatus which permitted the eye to see
further than anyone else had ever seen before, all the way
to the distant galaxies. Whether the eye emanated light
or whether light was drawn into the eye, the eye could
now see further and further into the ancient regions of
the past – through this ingenious device –

For which Galileo was summarily condemned –
Forced to recant.

The Sun goes round the Earth, he said. He bowed
his head. Inquisitors around him, ready to send him
away for execution.

Antiquity was correct, and the Church.

(Galileo later recanted his recantation.)

The layered museum was like a dream, in which people
came and went, from room to room, then vanished into the
depths of space.

(**l**) We were standing by a portrait of Robert Grosseteste,
who took his knowledge from Aristotle –

From Arabian scholars –

From long-lost magicians of nether-realms who
could no longer be summoned even with the most
advanced spells –

'Yes, Robert Grosseteste,' said Mortimer. 'A central figure in the medieval era.'

Robert Grosseteste looked severe and slightly haunted. As if he had a premonition. Or, as if his stomach pained him.

(**ɯ**) Roger Bacon's flying machine, a full-size replica, recreated from his original plans. A sail, ballasted by floating balls. A floating pendulum, coursing through the clouds.

'Incredible,' said Mortimer. 'Of course, it doesn't actually fly.'

(**n**) You might faint at the historical invention of these mechanical magicians.

(**o**) I was already feeling light-headed. The museum of so many layers, which were not yet concluded.

(**p**) My eyes fired out light, and light streamed into my head. And the dust was voluble, it squeaked.

(**q**) Amidst the squeak I heard Mortimer saying, 'Of course, our museum is not complete. Even the past, we cannot represent. And then the current epoch moves too swiftly. And then there is the Future – a great blank space, before us. Always. And when it is not before us, then it is no longer the future.'

We had arrived at the penultimate floor, and a sign said: THE PREVAILING MYSTERY IS LIGHT ...

(**r**) Newton said: *as Stones by falling upon Water put the Water into an undulating motion, and all Bodies by percussion excite vibrations in the air: so the rays of Light, by impinging on any*

refracting surface, excite vibrations in the refracting or reflecting
medium or substance, and by exciting them agitate the solid parts
of the refracting or reflecting body, and by agitating them cause
the body to grow warm or hot . . .

He also said that light consists of rays, and coloured
rings . . . that light passes through the long-gone Ether.

(8) Thomas Young, a Quaker, built on Newton's work
in the early nineteenth century. Thus, he used the word
'undulation', in preference to 'vibration', and he believed
in the existence of a plastic ether and the undulations
caused by luminous bodies.

He saw waves dispersing in deep water, and applied this vision to his undulatory theory of light . . .

(**t**) Using silver chloride-treated paper beneath coloured slabs of glass, mica and gems, Mary Somerville conducted experiments on the Sun's 'chemical rays'. On the grounds of her biological sex, she was not allowed to trouble the Royal Society with her work, so her husband, William, submitted her paper entitled, 'On the Magnetizing Power of the More Refrangible Solar Rays'. The distinguished authorities made him a fellow . . .

(**u**) Later in the nineteenth century, Augustin Cauchy was concerned with internal stress. Like Young, he imagined the ether as the medium responsible for light. The ether was as tangible, as true, as the sea.

(**v**) Soon after, the French polymath Jules-Henri Poincaré decided that the ether was not real at all.

(**w**) Mortimer was moving away. Besides, the history was partial, he explained. 'The final floor, above, is always empty, to represent what we do not know, what lies beyond.'

'Ingenious,' I said.

'Waste of space,' said Mortimer. 'But, I don't make the decisions.'

He was the tenant, not the owner, he said, as we walked into another room, with huge windows, and a misty view of Swinbrook Lane – Gothic turrets, gargoyles braying at the clouds. The mechanical magicians were waiting for us on the penultimate floor. They had taken a short break from their work, but they couldn't talk for long. They had to anticipate the future, before it became the present and then slipped into the perpetual darkness of the Past.

(**x**) 'Professor McConnell. Professor Glamorgan. Professor Agnew. Professor Strayte,' Mortimer was saying. I saw them first as an array of corduroy limbs. This was clearly unfair, a wild generalisation. Professor Strayte looked portly and eminent. Professor McConnell was younger, slightly irascible, with auburn hair. She was not even wearing corduroy, not a scrap! Professor Glamorgan had curly black hair, rubicund features. His corduroy was stained and torn, a deliberate or accidental refusal of formality. Professor Agnew was the youngest of them, with red hair and a sardonic expression. He was typing something into a computer. He glanced up, nodded, then resumed.

They stood on the shoulders of the past, they teetered on the brink of the future. Mortimer handed me over. He was going back downstairs, again, he said. No no, I mustn't get up. I shook his hand and thanked him. Nervous and hurried, he went away, tugging on his ear.

(**y**) The Professors told me their prevailing theories, as I nodded politely.

'The universe is incalculable by contemporary instruments, so it is the instruments that must change.' – Professor Strayte.

'There is no such thing as the present, in terms of clock time; it ends as soon as it has begun. And all we have is clock time.' – Professor McConnell.

'On the contrary, clock time is a phenomenal illusion, though a useful one.' – Professor Glamorgan.

'Time is intrinsic but the way we measure it is not.' – Professor Strayte.

'Neither is intrinsic. You are in the grip of an illusion.' Professor Glamorgan.

'It is easy to castigate the tangible as illusory; harder to discern the reality of the tangible.' – Professor Strayte.

In the midst of this, already, it was clear that Professor Agnew didn't say much. He was still typing. When I asked what he was doing, he explained that he was chirruping in the cyber-ether, the world within which everything must move, though it is invisible.

'The parallel intangible,' said Professor Strayte.

'We must not accord reality to that which is fundamentally a construct,' said Professor Glamorgan.

'In existence I conduct my experiments,' said Professor McConnell. 'My life is empirical fact.'

When I mentioned that I had known Solete, they all fell silent and even Agnew even stopped typing and looked at me.

'He loved the museum. Charted it and mapped it. It made him smile,' said Glamorgan. 'The illusions of yesteryear. The disappearance of everything that we once held to be indelible. Disappearance as the norm.'

'We must vanish, mustn't we?' said McConnell. She turned to me, so I nodded politely. 'And yet, Solete's work will survive. That's the wonderful thing. And why we constructed our museum.'

'But it hasn't survived,' I said. 'That's precisely the

problem. It's not there. Anywhere. It's vanished, in fact. Along with Solete.'

This made them mutter. McConnell looked pretty irritable. 'You've lost his great work?'

'No no, not lost. Never found.'

'Tantamount to lost, I'd say.' McConnell wasn't ceding the point. 'And it's really outrageous. Poor man. Did a rival steal it? Before you got there! You should have persuaded him to hand it over, before he died.'

'But perhaps Solete handed it over himself?' said Glamorgan.

'Would anyone else know?' I asked.

That set them on a course of earnest speculation. Some people might know, but it was not quite certain who they might be.

Agnew explained that Solete often came there and that he interrogated them about their research. Strayte, for example, was researching the origins of the universe. Contemporary systems of analysis were inadequate but they were hopeful new methods would emerge in his lifetime. Glamorgan believed that time was non-uniform, that only when we dispensed with Newtonian theories of analysis would we stand a chance of perceiving reality as it really is. Really. And in truth. McConnell believed that time began again and again, over and over and there was not one big bang but many. Infinite numbers of big bangs and, therefore, infinite numbers of possible universes, and one universe might just be very slightly different from another. Just in minuscule elements, barely noticeable to someone who – improbably – dropped in from another universe. You would just discern the slight anomalies, and nothing else. The people, the places, the basic elements might be the same, just very minor distinctions.

'Nonsense,' said Strayte. 'Complete gibberish. McConnell's theory takes a mathematical possibility and suggests reality proceeds in line with maths. But this is delusional, for the most part.'

'Or completely in line with reality,' said McConnell.

Agnew sat in the cyber-ether sunning himself and perceiving manifestations of futurity as they ebbed and flowed. 'I am interested in the virtual deliverance of the human condition,' said Agnew. 'I mean, that humans will be saved by our own creations, the cyber-ether pre-eminent among them.'

'If you stop calling it The Cyber-Ether and call it The Cyber-Matter then does it fundamentally change, or does it stay the same?' said McConnell. Agnew refused to write that down.

'How does the cyber-ether save us?' said Strayte.

'By fostering communication between the living and the dead,' said Agnew.

Everyone paused for a moment.

Agnew shrugged. 'In a sense,' he added. 'You should go and see the Society of the Universal Chrysanthemum. Solete was so whacked out on native perversity – sorry, but he was, and I liked the man – he could quite easily have given them his great work.'

'Those abject nutters?' said Strayte. 'Why not just tell her to go and score some dope from the nearest hippy and succumb to confusion?'

'I've already visited a hippy,' I said. 'And why do you academics always talk about dope?'

'The Society of the Universal Chrysanthemum aren't really hippies,' said Agnew. 'It's just a different way of being.'

'They believe in ascent and that mankind can fly,' said Strayte.

'Mankind *can* fly,' I said.

'They mean without mechanical assistance, obviously. Just spiritually. Or perhaps it's a big arm-flapping metaphor. That's how those kind of freaks normally justify deviations from sense,' said Strayte.

'Extraordinary claims need extraordinary proof,' said McConnell. She offered to take me to the ultimate floor: the Future.

'Shouldn't that be impossible?' I said.

'Symbolism is not literal,' she said. 'Don't you understand anything?'

'Obviously, I do. I understand some things,' I said. I was even slightly offended. She realised, and smiled an apology.

The ultimate floor was white, to symbolise – perhaps – the blank spaces on the metaphysical maps. Scientific regions as yet uncharted. Incantations as yet unspoken.

(ठ) The Zero of the Future. (Nothing Yet.)

So, we went from one empty room to another, each with a beautiful view of trees dividing the blank sky. I was trying to explain to McConnell that I didn't entirely understand. I had been with Cassavetes. She shrugged, she had no idea who Cassavetes was. Solete's various friends had not exactly mixed. They were incoherent, which seemed to have been his point. Or, he moved freely among them, but they refused to acknowledge each other. Where, for example, was Hypatia of Alexandria?

'Yes, yes,' said McConnell. 'No need to worry about her. She's down there. It's just, there's so much clutter. Not everything is immediately obvious. One good thing about the future: there's nothing here. But, another good thing: we know that soon there will be.'

'But the future goes down, doesn't it?' I said. 'As soon as it is. It can't be here, once it is, it automatically has to go below.'

That didn't bother her at all. 'Of course,' she said. 'Everything goes down. Rivers go downstream. And the virtual clock ticks down. And –'

'Hot air rises?'

'Until it cools, and then descends.'

McConnell didn't know where the *Field Guide* was. Her colleagues didn't know either. Back at the table of present findings, they said they were bemused. The situation was not certain.

'But,' said Agnew. 'It will be. One day.'

Monument of serenity, I thought.

I passed Mortimer at the gate, who wasn't serene at all. He was twitching and emanating a general atmosphere of deep uncertainty. But that was why he was right down, on the lowest floor, I assumed. He was in the depths, knowing almost nothing, that was his role. Not to know. And therefore, to permit.

I waved goodbye to Mortimer, who limped away. Then I walked onto Banbury Road again. My only lead was the Society of the Universal Chrysanthemum. At least that meant I didn't have to prevaricate.

I walked west, towards the Isis.

John Locke, the seventeenth-century philosopher, wrote his name as Lock. He was a mechanical magician long ago; I had seen a portrait of him on an early floor of the museum. He was a fellow of Aristotle Hall, and he kept his deepest thoughts concealed from others. He was known for personal secrecy. A contemporary, Humphrey Prideaux, described him thus:

'Not a word ever drops from his mouth that discovers any thing of his heart within . . . He seems to be a man of very good converse, and that we have of him with content; as for what else he is he keeps it to himselfe, and therefore troubles not us with it nor we him.' He was a veritable 'master of taciturnity.'

When Locke was in the middle of a project he would let no one enter his chamber.

Locke eventually pronounced his view of reality, and he suggested that we are born empty, and vacant. A taciturn poet, he used the image of the blank sheet of paper. We garner knowledge from sense experience, from perceiving the world beyond us. Yet, if perception is unreliable, and mysterious itself, then how can we be certain that our knowledge of the world is anything other than a personal illusion?

In silence, Locke passes across Aristotle meadow, towards the Isis. Geese are honking on the banks, and cows rustle through the grass. The Isis is still; it is a cold January day. Locke sees the world as a blank page, but as soon as we are born, impressions strike us, and are inscribed. Our personalities are created by experiences alone. There is nothing that precedes us: no intrinsic self, or neo-Platonic realm in which we are all-knowing. We are born without preconceptions, and we must gradually apprehend the world. We ascend from the beginning, the lowest point, to the heights of knowledge. Locke believed, faithfully, in progress. The child is blank. Life is a process of accumulation, from an original point, far below. From nothing to something, and then, we return, to nothing again.

Yet, Locke had high hopes for the afterlife; the knowledge gained in life was, apparently, perpetual. Perhaps that was how he would have understood the Future, the blank spaces at the top of the museum.

Heaven as a series of white rooms.

○ ○ ○

VIII

The Society of the Universal Chrysanthemum

Light is the natural agent that stimulates sight and makes things visible. The world is illuminated, and, thus, we see. Visible light, we might continue, is electromagnetic radiation whose wavelength falls within the range to which the human retina responds, i.e. between about 390 nm (violet light) and 740 nm (red). White light consists of a roughly equal mixture of all visible wavelengths, which can be separated to yield the colours of the spectrum, as was first demonstrated conclusively by Newton. In the twentieth century it has become apparent that light consists of energy quanta called photons that behave partly like waves and partly like particles. The velocity of light in a vacuum is 299,792 km per second.

Mortimer had given me a pamphlet, representing the latest mechanical theories of light. Or thereabouts. Something that was regarded as almost certain. I was reading it and trying to understand. Solete had gone into the darkness and taken his secrets with him. He had left some joke clues. Or perhaps they were serious. The further joke was that I couldn't tell. Then I had visited his monument of serenity. I was trying to follow the path, or force the clues to fit events. Sometimes I believed that he was mocking me. But that was grandiose, in itself.

Solete, or the mechanical magicians, had sent me back to the river again. The Society of the Universal Chrysanthemum was in the far north, just before the Isis flowed beyond the remit of the city. I walked through residential gargoyle mansions, and over a bridge towards a muddy river path. The city was beset by water, mired in a marsh.

This perplexed the clerics, and made them cough. Today the mist was full of broken sunlight. I passed an ancient water meadow, frost-whitened. I tried to call Yorke but he wasn't answering. Then I was angry with him, because he had offended me first. O'Donovan, instead, had left a message, asking me to call him. But I didn't feel like speaking to O'Donovan.

The silver river twined past fallen tree trunks, and matted stretches of frozen ground. Willows dangled their branches in the water. The sun flared behind clouds and then abruptly dwindled. At a weir, the river spat out spray. I walked into the grounds of a large, half-ruined house, its garden running down to the water. The Society of the Universal Chrysanthemum was apparently established here, in this Tudor building. Once, visitors might have arrived by boat, from London, to visit a great lord. These days, the place was crumbling, the timbers were bent, the roof was full of holes. I wandered around the melancholy building, looking for someone who might be able to explain what the chrysanthemum was and why it was universal.

A door had been left ajar, so I went inside, calling, 'Hello? Hello?'

I had entered an interior courtyard, with a small fountain. There were doors opening off the courtyard, and the roof was open to the cold white sky. Beside the fountain was a small spindly tree, and on the walls were paintings representing animals and plants. A moon was drawn with all its stages superimposed. There was a man drawn as a series of pictures, in which the elements changed – different aspects of his past had been selected in each picture and

were seen to determine a different present and a different
future. Every image was laced with echoes, possibilities.

A sunken-eyed woman appeared. She had copious
quantities of matted black hair, twisted beautifully into
thick plaits, and she was wearing a long red dress. I
explained why I was there, and followed her into a con-
servatory, with hanging plants and wicker chairs. She told
me to take a seat, and went to speak to someone else. No
sooner had I sat down than a man arrived, who explained
that he was not the head of their society, but he would
try to answer my questions. He was a moderately plump,
barrel-chested character, wearing a black suit. He was
called Michael, he explained. He introduced me to his
wife, Thea, the woman who had greeted me at first. There
was a stillness to the place which quite distressed me.

I asked what the Universal Chrysanthemum was, and
Thea said that it was pointless to explain, because at the
point at which you understood the name
you knew it anyway.

'You are within, and therefore, you don't need to know.'
That clearly didn't help at all.

They offered me some tea and I said yes, politely. I felt the
enterprise was already futile and I should go as soon as I
could. We went into another muralled room, where the
prevailing theme was the seasons:

The rise and fall of leaves –

The trees in bloom and then becoming golden and rus-
set and generally autumnal.

Then the dying of the year, the stripped and plaintive
branches.

'Lord Priddy is the leader of this society,' said Thea.

'Another blissfulle patriarche,' I said. They looked at me with sorrow in their eyes, and poured more tea.

Psychotropic tea.

I hadn't even considered the possibility.

Events thereafter were a little strange.

The Society of the Universal Chrysanthemum has many mysteries that doubtless remain hidden, to me, but at least I can say that, if you do pay them a visit then don't, in any sense, drink the tea.

As soon as I had drunk the first cup, Thea told me her name was really Thys, and Michael told me that the thing I must absolutely remember was *Id It oh*. I was trying to get him to clarify what the hell he meant by this, but he just repeated it again.

Id It oh

There's nothing more infuriating than someone repeating a phrase over and over again when you have expressly asked him to make himself more intelligible. But after a while Michael stopped repeating this meaningless phrase and instead became abruptly and quite surprisingly meaningful. He said:

How can one awaken? How can one escape this sleep?

Meanwhile, a tall thin man in a white suit entered the room. The murals were going through their seasons, but the pace was getting a little frenetic. I wasn't really sure why the murals had to move in this eager spinning way, as if they were urging the seasons on, years were rising and falling, time was passing. Now the man in the suit introduced himself as Lord Priddy and said, 'I hear you knew Solete?'

'Yes, yes I did,' I said. I was making a big effort to stop the room spinning. In the midst of such centrifugal force, I said, 'I was trying to find his *Field Guide.*'

'His great work?' said Priddy.

Yes, said the trees. I said yes. Michael said:

Id It oh

– until I blocked him out again.

'Right,' said Priddy. 'Well. We often discussed his great work. Often. Solete was a valued visitor. He always had his own idiosyncratic take on things, wouldn't you say? Made him different from everyone else.'

'As idiosyncrasy does, indeed,' I said.

'And he talked a lot about where he would put the work, so it was safe, when he died,' said Lord Priddy.

'Yes, did he? Well, it would be wonderful if you – I mean.

Where was I?'

'Did you drink the tea?' said Priddy.

'Yes, yes, I did.'

'Did they ask you before they gave it to you?'

'No, they just went straight ahead.'

'That was very foolish of them. But they are foolish.'

Thys looked foolish. Michael said, Id It oh.

'I can only apologise. You should be prepared to travel now,' said Priddy.

'Shall I go back home?'

'No no, just wait here. Just remember, if it eats you, it's not actually real.'

'What's not actually real?'

He didn't reply.

'If what eats me?' I said.

He didn't reply to that either. He was completely unforthcoming. 'Can you hear me?' I said again, beginning to panic.

'And whatever you do, just keep calm.'

Priddy vanished. Everyone vanished. The murals kept spinning through the years. And time passed, aeons. Ages were expended as I sat there trying not to panic. I was alone. And suddenly the walls were dissolved by the passing of time, and I was blasted across the universe. It happened incredibly fast. I heard the distant cries of civilisation, but they were so far behind me, I could barely remember where I had come from. The stars were blurred into a glittering line and I saw the sun, a boiling fireball, emanating impossible heat towards me. Now I passed through nebulae and dust clouds and all the dust sparkled as I was flung further and further into – the body of a giant chrysanthemum, which was the fixed point of All Time.

Everything stopped. I stuck my head out of the chrysanthemum, and looked around. I could see back to my own galaxy but it was extremely far away. I saw it as a sequence of small black dots, moving around the pinprick light of the sun. Beyond me I could see to galaxies unknown, great clusters of stars, dense clouds of gas. Blackness, redness, whiteness, and hot heat –

Ghost stars, lost stars, black holes then spun webs of nothing, dark matter, reams of nothingness and empty space and then the scattered luminescence of stars, so many

billions of lights. So beautiful! So insane! I realised now the chrysanthemum was not moving but all space was instead moving around it, every star, every galaxy. It turned so fast that I felt dizzy. It was spinning round and round me as I sat in the heart of everything. Lights and shadows, spinning faster and faster, and each time reality turned it became just somehow less real, and more like a vast region of formlessness, everything elided –

I was trying to explain to the chrysanthemum that I really wanted to leave, but no meaningful sounds came out, just inchoate gibberish, and, anyway, who knew what language this flower spoke, and whether it spoke any language at all. For a while I was wondering quite seriously how best to communicate with a gargantuan flower and then with a jolt I realised this was completely insane and it was impossible to communicate with a flower at all, however large it was, and even if it was the focal point of the entire universe. Meanwhile all the galaxies, stars, nebulae, realities, were still moving around the chrysanthemum, and now they seemed even to be accelerating faster and faster, as if the whole of reality had gone into hyperdrive. In the midst, in the focal point, I was mumbling and laughing with nerves and incipient panic and just when I was about to throw up, the flower threw up instead and in fact threw me up – I was jettisoned with great force and, once repulsed, I began to fall, swiftly, all the way down – down – beyond – all the way below and down – and into the great pit of – the blackness of pure space. All was silent – my fall was very fast, and I thought about screaming for help but then it was impossible to imagine who could feasibly help me and besides I was falling so quickly

I couldn't even open my mouth. Then with a great sucking sound the earth received me again, dragged me back –

To this moment.

Here.

Now.

I was sitting on a bench, in the mural room, and Lord Priddy was offering me another drink.

'No way,' I mumbled. 'No.'

'This will help,' he said. 'I'm very sorry. They mistook you for someone else.'

The new drink was also tea but, I hoped, not the sort of tea that projected you across the universe into the heart of a giant chrysanthemum.

'I saw the flower,' I said. 'I sat in it and looked around and then it spat me out, back here again.'

'Then all is well. Some people get eaten. Metaphorically, as I tried to emphasise before. I was a little – startled.'

Lord Priddy was a tall, friendly man, with thick blond hair, broad shoulders and a handsome, slightly scrunched up face, as if he had once been smacked firmly between the eyes with a cricket bat. He might have been about fifty. His white suit was crumpled and, quite inevitably, he had a yellow chrysanthemum in his buttonhole.

'Are you *actually* a lord?' I said.

'Not in the formal parliamentary sense. But in the sense of our own order, then yes I am the most high lord.'

'You're in charge?'

'Yes.'

'Did you know Solete?'

'Very well, yes.'

'Did he drink the tea?'

'Occasionally. He was more interested in assessing the effects of the tea on other people.'

'So he watched?'

'Yes.'

'What are the effects of the tea?'

Lord Priddy explained that the effects, from worst to best, were:

Frenzy – in which the initiate became violently agitated and fell to the ground writhing and screaming
> (The chrysanthemum had eaten them. They were therefore not ready for the next stage.)

Stupor – in which the initiate became essentially catatonic and sometimes fell to the floor with their limbs rigid
> (In this state, the universe had not turned around them. The universe of the chrysanthemum had got stuck. The initiate was therefore not ready for the next stage.)

Indeterminate physical posture – in which the initiate displayed an expression of bewilderment
> (They had travelled to the chrysanthemum but could not gain access to the heart of the flower. The initiate was therefore not ready for the next stage.)

Mild agitation – in which the initiate stared wildly, seemed not to understand whatever they perceived, and descended into unmitigated confusion
> (They had travelled to the heart of the chrysanthemum and gained access to the interior of the flower but

were then violently spat back to earth again. This was
my condition. I was also not ready for the next stage.)

'But it wasn't bad,' said Lord Priddy. 'You might even get
to the lower stages of enlightenment, next time.'

There will be no next time, I thought.

Priddy was telling me about the lower stages of enlightenment, their worth depending on the length of habitation
in the chrysanthemum and so on and eventually the initiate
arrived at the ideal state – beatific calm and splendour – in
which they sallied forth to the heart of the chrysanthemum
and experienced the totality of all existence, their own and
that of humanity, and that of the universe – and were duly
enlightened. Therefore, they gained access to the inner
sanctum of the society of the Universal Chrysanthemum.

'Solete's observations, did he say they were for his great
work?' I asked.

'In a sense.'

'In the sense that?'

'Everything was related to this work.'

'Did he ever say where he was putting the work? Or
what he was doing with it?'

'No.'

Now Thys and Michael were hovering at the edge of the
room, looking embarrassed. I tried to wave at them, to sug-
gest that things were fine really, but found my limbs were
shaking. I couldn't align my intentions with my actions.

'Do come back and see us again,' said Lord Priddy. I
tried to nod politely, but my head was shuddering even as
I moved it, and, with a clumsy wave, I tried to walk away.

The journey through the garden took me hours, it seemed. It seemed the birds reeling around me and fluttering onto the trees were moving very slowly too, as if they might any moment fall from the skies.

Lord Priddy was saying, 'You should try the quantum realm. It's in the far south where the Cherwell flows into the Isis, and one river drinks the other. Solete often went there, too.'

'The quantum realm?'

'It looks like an aeroplane that went headfirst into the bank of the river.'

I nodded again, then half-stepped, half-fell. I think Lord Priddy waited as I staggered away, but by then my eyes were closing, the sky was mottled with dark clouds. I moved into the gathering darkness. There was a lull as the river ebbed and gurgled along beside me, and the red sun slid towards the horizon. I had missed a call from Anthony. He had finally broken his silence. In the message he sounded nervous and slightly plaintive. *Which part of the river are you on? Let me know.*

When I called him back, he was in a tutorial.

'I'm afraid I can't really talk. What's happening?' he said.

'Things have become just slightly counterintuitive. It's like the day, or reality, is being held by someone who keeps shaking. Reality has palsy.'

'I'm sorry about whatever I should have said when we last met,' he said.

'I'm sorry about what I actually said.'

'Are you alright?'

I wasn't even sure about that. I looked out at pale tracts

of water. The limits of the river seemed to be indeterminate. Trees overhanging, drenched roots. The distant sound of cars, whining along a major road. The chrysanthemum, and the monolith.

'I have to go to the quantum realm, apparently. Not now. Tomorrow. Too late today. I only just got out of the chrysanthemum,' I said. 'Or, really, it spat me out.'

'Is that a metaphor?'

'Too confusing to explain on the phone.'

'I'm going to the Parkland after work. Shall we meet there?'

'Alright. Yes.'

I hung up because my head ached. Then my entire being ached, I thought how strange it was to be flung across the universe. I felt bruised, as if I had genuinely vaulted across light years and collided with a gargantuan flower, but there was no physical reason for my agony. My shoulders were in spasms. The trees hung limply in the water, sad willows, dipping their branches. My teeth were chattering. I thought about Solete, how I had known so little about him. I had been too mired in grief to realise that he was in mourning too – for his life, for his youth, for his beloved dead. I realised that his routine was fixed and purposeful, that he shunned the college and went to the café, perhaps because no one knew him there.

Solete told me once that his father walked with one foot slightly twisted to the side, having been injured in the First World War. Solete was brought up in Oxfordshire, and, though he went to fight in another World War, he returned, in the end, to the cold white stone, the city of shadows.

Rather than taking his place in line with contemporary orthodoxies, Solete perhaps believed that the arrangement of finite parts, if managed most precisely, might yield some change in the vast and invisible portion of the universe.

Or, it might not.

Mist swirled across the dying sun. Thousands of birds, reeling above me, forging vast circles, round and round, so the mist was flecked with all these swirling spots of blackness, and the sky swirled. There were geese lining the banks of the river, and suddenly, in one great cluster, they ascended and flew directly towards me. I even thought they would collide with me, I ducked and heard their wings thudding directly above my head, their honking and bellowing! Shadowy forms surging towards the moon, and the circling flocks of smaller birds, everything swirling, black shapes against the whiteness, and melancholy cries. I watched slow-moving herds of cattle, meandering towards the river. A flurry, the sound of hooves, and wild horses cantered furiously across the meadow, faster and faster, tossing their manes, whinnying, coming ever closer to me, whinnying, in a line, faster and closer until they were upon me – for a moment I thought I should run but then I was fixed where I stood, too terrified to move. They passed either side of me, their eyes shining in the moonlight, their crazy ecstatic whinnying and then a last frenzy of commotion and the smell of sweat and straw as my heart pounded in my chest – and – then – one horse collided with me, so I fell. Dimly, I heard the meadow still echoing with the sound of hooves.

Blankness perhaps. For a while? And hard to tell . . .

Yet, the sky was still full of birds, moving in perfect synchronicity. Whirling clouds dimmed the stars, I was shaking with wonder and disoriented entirely. Everything faded into silence, as if there were nothing around me at all. I stood carefully, brushing myself down in a perfunc-tory way. I was coated in cold mud. The clouds devoured the moon and I walked in perfect blackness, my hands outstretched, shivering and trembling, talking to myself. *Just to the edge of the blackness,* I said. *Only the edge, then the city lights begin.* I began to think I was dead and that the horse had trampled me and now I was in the afterlife or underworld, and this was death, to walk in darkness across a grassy meadow, in pure unbridled blackness, nothingness all around . . .

In my confused state I became completely convinced that this was absolutely true and I was absolutely dead. I was terrified for a while and then I began to feel almost relieved, that there was an afterlife, that I was in it! That the busi-ness of mortal consciousness was over – though now I had to contend with a new variant of consciousness – whatever it was! My heart was beating, an illusion I thought. Why to be a body, in the afterlife? How to be? I wondered? I peered into the blackness and it seemed that I could discern sub-categories of blackness, shapes that might be human. Or, I wondered if they might be memories, if I was in a liminal realm where thoughts became embodied, and drifted along beside you. But how would anything be embodied, in a non-corporeal realm? It was so strange, and I walked forwards, not knowing where forwards conveyed me, and these shadowy half-forms accompanied me. The ground beneath my feet was hard and firm, cold mud. This comforted me, and I tried to listen for the sound of horses, the cawing of birds, but – nothing!

Blankness!

For a long time, ages, I walked with my hands out-stretched. Shadows surged, and dwindled. I roamed through emptiness until finally I blinked and hardly trusted what I saw –

The timorous glow –

The sulphur-stained city –

Shadowy old turrets and all the memories, traces, mirages –

So I was alive, after all!

o o o

On the Nature
of Shadows

At the Parkland, the gates were shut, so I crawled over the wall, fell roughly into the brambles, scrambled out again. I wandered onto the path, dazed and rubbing a bruised elbow. In the Bronze Age, tribes had worshipped here. Brittonic druids wandered the forests, intoning to their gods. Now it was silent and deserted, apart from Yorke, who was standing like a prisoner, his arms rigidly at his sides. His hair was tousled, as if, once more, he had forgotten to comb it. Blond and pale-skinned, he was almost as bleached as the landscape around him. A ghost man, in search of historical vapours. Once more, he was under-clad.

'I'm sorry,' he said, as soon as I reached him. 'Again.'

'That's alright,' I said, trying to become as reasonable as possible. As quickly as possible. 'I'm sorry I said you were a fantasist.'

'It's undoubtedly a just charge,' he said. 'In a sense, that's my job.'

'I'm sure it's not.'

'At least, in so far as what I do is a job.'

'You sound like Solete.'

'I have a lot of sympathy for Solete. I mean, beyond the obvious.'

We began to walk along a dusty path, into a further region of prevailing whiteness. As if to cement our moment of accord, he said, in a confiding tone: 'I've always hated coats. You're too hot, you take them off, you're too cold; you put them on, you're too hot. So, you may as well be one or the other. Perpetually. In winter, I am perpetually too cold.'

'Even unto hypothermia?'

'I've never been found rigid by the side of the road.'

I was still quite dislocated from the objects around me. Tea, clouding my senses. My dream visions seemed more real than the Parkland. I tried to listen as Anthony told me about the henge. 'Pagan ground,' he was saying. 'These things get lost. This site was lost for a thousand years. Deliberate camouflage by the Christian Church, in part. They must have built the clerical colleges here on purpose, trying to sanctify the heathen site. Nightingale Hall with its massive chapel. You know, the early Church, it was always doing that sort of thing.' He waved his arm, vaguely. I found I could barely respond.

'Are you alright?' he said, turning suddenly towards me.

'I drank too much tea. Then, for a while, I thought I had died.'

'From drinking tea?' He looked at me as if this was a *non sequitur*. He simply needed the full picture. I was going to explain, as soon as I had ascertained just precisely what – the full picture – might be – but he started speaking again.

'It's a circular site, a great zero. The sacred eternal number. The mystery of nothing. That clue – *no matter*.'

'Is nothing mysterious?'

He ignored me. 'You'd expect a place like this to be haunted by uneasy spirits.'

'I don't believe in that kind of thing.' At least, not usually, I thought. These things have to be suppressed!

'Really it was genocide,' Anthony was saying. 'Danes. They were resident Danes, they'd lived their lives in England. Peacefully, you know. But suddenly, one day, in the early eleventh century, the English king said to his subjects, go out and massacre them all. He was tired of the raids along the coast, Vikings, you know, the rest. He issued an edict. They must have gone to Nightingale Hall, to seek sanctuary. It was just a chapel then, nothing more, we're talking about the period before the university was established. No scholar-clerics. And they got hemmed in, trapped, those poor Danes, they were attacked, maimed, beaten – they ran for the chapel, begged for mercy. But the people had their edict from the king and so they burnt the chapel down, the Danes were trapped inside. All of them – men, women, children – burnt to death.'

'That's really awful,' I said. 'How appalling –'

Anthony shrugged.

As we walked, I became progressively more confused. That was unfortunate because I had been fairly confused when we began the walk. I had just returned from an unsolicited psychotropic experience. It was perhaps tactless of Anthony to start talking about uneasy ghosts and massacres. As we walked, branches scraped on other branches, squeaking and even at times wailing. But branches do not wail, of course. I was fully aware that my senses were out of synch with the world around me. The measurements of trees are stern and imperious but usually they are fixed. They do not shift as you approach, and become larger, more imposing, and surge their forms towards you, as if they are beckoning, onwards. Now everything was curled, every wizened bush, every blade of grass. Frilled ivy on the buildings. I shivered. Anthony stopped, again, and said, 'Are you sure you're alright? Do you want to sit down?'

I really didn't want to stop at all. The frills were just too – frilly! I wanted to get beyond them and into a place where frills were not. Or, where frills were not so – frilly. I shook my head. My thoughts were tangled, as if the frills had extended across my mind, as if frills were psychic knotweed, some tangling agent, that confused thought –

I tried again. Thoughts cannot be bound in knotweed. Metaphors cannot be literal. Frills cannot – engulf your mind –

Clearly!

I became aware that Anthony had put a hand on my arm, guiding me – the frills beneath. 'Are you cold?' he said.

'Not the cold,' I managed to say back to him, but now the park was surging towards me, each shadowy tendril, each patch of darkness. Yorke moved away, I heard him shivering – but the sound was immense, as if it was echoing across the park. I thought I saw people moving between the trees, their long black robes rustling on the frozen ground. I thought I saw Hypatia, being dragged away! But that was just the tea again. My mind was undone! I was mired in uncertainty and then I heard this shivering sound behind me, so I broke into a run. Wherever I was, it seemed best to keep away from such a sound. With that firmly in mind, I began to hurry. Anthony approved of haste, so he started walking even faster.

'Tell me more about the henge,' I said. I was trying to return to the tranquil glades of murderous history. At least that was all established fact. Something to cling onto, surely?

'Ah well,' said Anthony. 'So, the poor murdered Danes

were tossed into the henge. By then, you know, the Christian church had taken hold and so these henges were just used for rubbish. The zero – the circle – was at the edge of Oxford, at the time. You can imagine it – pretty ghoulish – the carts moving along, piled with the ragged dead and then these grey-faced workers who had the doleful task of throwing bodies into the pit. That's all the henge was to them – by then – just an open grave – there were no traces, no earthworks visible. It went round in this great circle, but that didn't mean anything in the Dark Ages. They'd wiped out the past, jettisoned it entirely.'

'So they weren't curious? They didn't try to – work out – what the hell it was?'

'No, they just filled it in – with rubbish, with unholy corpses, the bodies of their enemies. No one knew about it, until last year. And that was a complete accident! They were digging the foundations of a new student block, and suddenly, they hit a skull. Just one at first. But one is bad enough! The whole thing was shut down, no more mechanical diggers, they all had to resort to chopsticks, little picks, you know. Full-on archaeology. The contractors were weeping tears of blood. But they found another skull, then another. Then five more, then a load of skeletal limbs. Imagine! The surprise. Horror, even. They kept counting up tragic skeletal remains. Then they realised, these bodies had their heads smashed in, they had been pummelled and beaten and spiked with swords; they had died amidst great violence and suffering. They were burnt. They had discovered the scene of an ancient crime.'

Yorke was moving more and more quickly, so I began to jog, to keep pace with him. My feet pounding on the frilly

frosted grass, trampling the tendrils, and I thought of the
rhythmic sound of our footsteps as they echoed below — far
below! Anthony was continuing, as if we were on a pleas-
ant stroll, and he was gently illuminating the stuff around
us. He said: 'The positive aspect of all this historical
slaughter was that they discovered the grave was strangely
shaped. It seemed to be part of a circular formation. It
went on, and on. They started digging it up and before
they knew it they had found the henge. Such chance! No
one knew, before that, that the park was an ancient Druidi-
cal site.'

Around us, mist-blank space, the shadow glade. Cold air
filled my lungs and we walked for a while in silence, puffing out smoke.

Then —

'This sacred circle, running round the park,' said
Anthony. 'It's quite neat. If you think about it. And the
circle in general. The rivers, making a circle round the city
— two rivers, combining to circumnavigate the city, so it's
almost an island. So the henge is a circle within a circle.'

'*No matter it was nothing,*' I said. 'But then, I'd wondered
if he just meant the future. The zero. If we've done that
one already.'

'No, I think it's the earthwork,' said Anthony. 'The
great zero. Eternal life.'

'The still point?'

The circle. The zero. Everything and nothing. And I was
befogged by tea and prevailing atmospheric mist. As we
crossed into the centre of the park — the centre of the henge —

each movement brought more and more shadowy frills
towards me, and it was impossible to tell, at times – where
the mist ended, and the cold park began. I could hear a
background hum, which seemed to be getting louder as
we walked. Anthony was hastening along, hands in his
pockets, habitual attitude of existential pallor. I wondered
what he even expected to find here. And why the frills were
massing towards me! Meanwhile the hum was outside, or
inside, my head. I couldn't tell!

'Is the *Field Guide* in the henge?' I said. 'Is that it? No
matter? In the nothing?'

'It's not *in* the henge,' said Anthony. 'The henge is
the neolithic channel that circumnavigates the park, the
spiritual ha-ha, if you like. It circumnavigates the park and
runs past Solete's former house and through Solete's former
college. The centre of the park is the centre of the henge
and therefore the site of maximum spiritual power. But of
course he didn't put the book in the henge. That would be
absurd!'

'But then, why are we doing this?'

'If we just wait then something might occur to us. A
revelation.'

'Of course,' I said. 'Fantastic idea, thanks so much.'

Anthony walked faster and faster. There was something
relentless about his pace. Of course, the cold, his general
hypothesis that coats were evil, or whatever his theory of
the coat. It wasn't quite the time for sartorial philosophy. I
understood. I didn't understand at all. Anything. Even
coats were becoming strange and controversial. I carried
on, and on, and I felt something like – resistance? My own?

Or, the mist was becoming turgid? We were approaching
the centre of the old earthworks, the place of maximum
power. If you believed that sort of thing, which I didn't.
And I assumed, neither did Anthony. But we were desperate. Everything else was increasingly intangible. Trees
rustled as we walked, and clouds moved slowly above the
towers of the city. Electricity hummed, or some other force
I couldn't begin to understand. The moon slid through the
mist, staining it silver. Another shadow leered towards me
– I recoiled! But it was nothing, of course. Another frill, a
tendril, and then I moved into another region of shadow,
I stepped into it, felt the cold air grip me. Reality came in
and out as if I was receiving it on an ancient radio. Crack-
ling on the wires. Intermissions of static.

Now Anthony faded into the mist and became engulfed.
I panicked, hurried to catch up with him.

'Don't go so far ahead,' I said.

'Why?' He sounded confused. 'We're nearly there.'

'Where?'

'The epicentre.'

'How can you tell?'

We both stopped.

'Oak ash and hawthorn,' said Anthony. 'In druidi-
cal times these were the sacred trees which indicated the
epicentre.'

We looked around. There were no trees. No druids.
Nothing but grass and frills and tendrils.

'So, times have moved on,' I said.

I was surprised to find Anthony lying on the cold
ground, spread-eagled, all the frills flattened beneath him.

'What are you doing?' I said. The question was insufficient. A pallid man, a pallid sky, a drowsy park where shadows surged, and something hummed, and everything was tinged with the residual effects of tea . . .

'Listening,' he said, his voice muffled.

'To what?'

He lay there for a long while, as I stood, outraged. Expectant, then thinking, *but what the hell am I expecting?*

'Wait.'

So Yorke was lost, I thought. As he lay there, frills biting at his ankles, with a more general suggestion that he was in total existential disarray, I thought – he's lost, and he didn't even drink the tea! It was hopeless trying to reason with him. So, I lay down beside him on the cold earth. My body was instantly cold, the frost crackled beneath me. I began to shiver, and then I heard a yet more sonorous hum, which seemed to come from – underground. The earth was febrile and surprisingly loud. Meanwhile, we listened. I listened to the hum and Yorke listened to whatever he was listening to as well. I was aware even as we listened that another sound was rising and even competing with the guttural hum. It was the wind, shaking the trees, so they began to bounce and reverberate, like strings on a lyre. Steadily, this eerie chorus rose above the hum.

My face was rigid with cold. Anthony stood, shaking his head. '*It was nothing.* There is nothing. Bloody hell!'

'I heard something, I thought.' I stood, aware that I was intensely cold.

'*No matter it was nothing*,' said Anthony. 'I meant that.

Maybe it means: nothing is not necessarily a bad thing. So, it doesn't matter if it was nothing. Don't worry. You know, embrace the zero. The great O. Don't try to fill it.'

'But it's full anyway,' I said. 'Your freaky Danes and then the shadows. All the frills. And besides, it's humming!'

Meanwhile the wind was making the trees bow and buck, so their song became louder and louder, as the branches danced and the shadows seemed to dance as well.

'Are you OK?' said Anthony.

'Yes, but you should have seen it. The chrysanthemum was so enormous it encompassed – the universe.'

'Which chrysanthemum?'

'The really really big one. The one in the middle of time and space.'

'Are you drunk?'

'No, it was psychotropic tea. At the Priddy man's place. A tea cult. I didn't realise.'

Into a rising storm, we walked. The roar and shout of the wind, tendril forms of the trees, jostling. We were blown out of the park by accelerating gusts of wind and then we were buffeted along the street, shadows jumping in the street lights, branches slapping the walls and occasional bangs as the wind blew something over. A mighty storm. We hurried, our heads bowed. Down one street, a wind tunnel, and then onto Nightingale Lane. Above us, a parapet of gargoyles, casting lurid shadows. Two petrified women, sleeping, side by side and always in their stupor. Above, the silver mist, the smothered moon. Anthony was walking so fast, I tried to tell him to slow down, but he kept walking onwards, and seemed not to hear me. Onwards, and then the blackness swallowed him.

There followed an unnerving moment, when I could only see frills and surging shadows. Everything else was fading at the edges – I had to focus! I broke into a run – shivering, stumbling. My mind was amazed and now my body seemed to have lost all sense of reasonable parameters as well. I kept saying mind mind mind and then I said body body body and then I began to laugh at such ridiculous words! What did they even mean? I was bowing over, laughing towards the frilly ground, but then I realised the frills had followed me from the park, and besides I heard something humming beside me, or around me, the hum greater and more sonorous than before, and all the birds crying in the trees, and all the frills beneath me and yet rising – surging – and I thought I might faint.

Then I saw Solete, but I was so floored by recent events that this failed even to surprise me.

He was walking slowly towards the river. He looked as I had last seen him – tall, stooped, wearing an immaculate suit. An atmosphere of reassuring calm.

'It's been very difficult, since you died,' I said.

'I'm sorry about that,' he said. He was very far away.
I had to raise my voice slightly. He was receding, even as
I spoke to him.

'Now I've lost Anthony.'

'That's alright,' he said. 'He'll be fine.'

'And what about you?'

I was trying to call him back but now I saw there was
nothing but the shadow of Nightingale Tower, the old
black river moving beneath, as the trees danced to these
fervent songs and bells tolled above. Darkly the river
meandered, dreamlike. The moon was mist-smothered
and the stars were barely there at all. I kept looking
around, I got scared by a cat jumping from a tree, I panted
out nervous breaths, my breath swallowed by the wind
and I felt as if I was fading too, everything was fading,
I ran, I stalled –

No one on the street. Cars slurring past, but that hardly
helped. I turned the corner, heart banging, I ran and the
night gulped, and I reached my door, thinking, oh someone, save me, but from what?

I was inside, breathing deeply – I slammed the door.

All that night I had crazy dreams. The storm hammered
on the windows, and the street was livid with sound and
fury, the trees hissing and shuddering. And I dreamed
that there was something dragging me out – into the swart
night –

Sliding blackness – sliding upwards –

Then – in my dream – I was flung abruptly into space.

It was like the chrysanthemum vision again except this time I was not in the heart of the cosmos, my dream flight was more local, and I remained above the old city. The clouds were surging around me, there was a low hum. In my dream the storm had died down and the sky was clear – it was beautiful up there, far above those streets – I'd trodden them so many times, but now they were like patterns of dark and light, the people forming clusters, shifting again and again –

I was paddling through the ether, moving somehow forwards – and beyond – the shadow city all below me, the chimneys puffing out their smoke, the shadows and the people moving from one dark place and into one more pool of light. Now I was moving towards a small house on an island –

Mesopotamia –

I saw the familiar place, old stone, edged around with blackness, Solete's house. He was nowhere to be seen, but in front of me was Robert Grosseteste. I was about to say something to him – but what? But then I realised, Grosseteste was watching someone else, someone I could now see, when I squinted into the gloom. Grosseteste was monochrome, the light was fading all around him, but the man he watched was standing within a cloud of frills, tendril shapes, and yet, within that cloud were shining forms, like fireflies glittering. And this man even seemed to conjure frills – to make them move – as I watched – as Grosseteste watched. And we watched him move his fingers through the air and now the frills formed into shapes – as if he was writing – words in the air –

They were in no language I could understand – but I

knew that I had to remember the shapes — in my dream I was absolutely sure that I must retain them precisely —

So I was staring and staring and trying to commit these shapes to memory —

كيفيات الإظلال

So many frills. Beautiful, snakelike forms. I didn't understand. And as for him! He wasn't making any progress either. He was staring at the shapes, this strange conjurer of frills, and all the firefly lights were glittering around him —

كيفيات الإظلال

Then the man looked up, as if he was about to speak to Robert Grosseteste and I assumed of course that Grosseteste would speak back to him but instead — Grosseteste began to turn — in my direction —

He was about to look towards me — I was about to say something to him —

Something like —

The wind tousling the reed banks, and ripples spreading on the dark water —

I woke into the harsh glare of the morning.

o o o

Ɔ

Priests of the
Quantum Realm

The city raised its chant, an ordinary hum of traffic and the grind of buses and people murmuring to each other but it sounded at times like

Burnished flower! Arise!

I shook my head. After the mild tribulations of the night, I felt it was important to keep a grip on things. Things must be gripped and kept exactly where they should be and where they usually are. I was to become a stalwart of reality. I would go and find the book, which was, after all, merely a book, and then I would return to ordinary life. The café. The museum. Work. The parameters of the Real and True.

It had gone a little too far. Poisoned tea and the accidental revelations of the night.

I blamed Yorke for much of it. Then I blamed myself.

I was out on the street again, and it was morning. So I walked. The sun had burnt away the mist, torched it with purgatorial fire. I thought, *and so I am released from the spell!* Then I realised this was all part of an irrational and anti-realist worldview. I had to stop all of this. There was, evidently and plainly, no spell. There had been a hiatus, when my logical mind had been drawn into the random enterprises of hippies and flower-worshippers and even perhaps Cassavetes was a druid. But this had nothing to do with anything. The weather was, as ever, as always. The weather always changes.

I had to remember. Rocks and stones do not have feelings. I was crossing the river. The blue sky was reflected in the sun-fired water. People were squinting in the sun. They

still had their phones at their faces, but now they said, it
was much better. Finally, a reprieve from the mist. Can't
complain, can you? And they didn't complain, they kept
walking, onwards, always – over the river and into the city,
where they dispersed.

I turned into Nightingale Hall. The Porter nodded
towards me again.

'Someone expecting you?' he said.

He waved me through.

Yorke was sitting in his room, hunched over. The curtains
were drawn, the floor was covered with little balls of
scrunched up paper. It seemed the man suffered from low
self-esteem. There were far too many books for his shelves,
and he had stacked the remainder in piles around the room.
Meanwhile he was at his desk, wearing another battered
suit. When I entered, he rose to his feet.

'Well,' he said. 'How are you feeling?'

'How are *you* feeling, more like?' I said.

'You were the one who was acting strangely, I would
have thought,' he said.

'I would have thought it was you,' I said.

'Would you really?'

'First you banged on about marauding Danes and then
you lay on the ground. For no apparent reason.'

'There was a reason. I was explaining it to you, but you
were so distracted,' he said.

'Well, the ambient hum was too loud, I couldn't hear
anything else.'

He gave me a strange look. Of course, it was a strange
thing to say. I had to remember. The strange versus the

not strange. The distinctions therein. Of course a great
hum had not reverberated around the misty park, and
ricocheted across the clouds. None of that was real.
I needed to create an indelible and certain system.

> REAL
> The day
> The street
> The people of the present

> UNREAL
> The night
> The hum
> The people of the past

On his desk, I saw a piece of paper. Something about it,
something frilly, drew my attention. He saw me looking,
and covered it with a book.

'Could I possibly have a look at that?' I said.

'Why?'

'Just – a whim.'

'Why are you acting like this?'

I was reaching towards the piece of paper when he
picked it up and handed it to me. It said –

كيفية اإلظالال

An incantation for dispersing shadows
(Alhazen of Cairo)

'Frills! But that's insane,' I said. 'And frankly unfair. I've
been trying to rationalise things, get them back into their
respective categories. Then – this!'

Now I lunged for the curtain and dragged it open,

much to Yorke's further consternation. He stood as if to say, what the hell? Yet, I was intent on this action and it transpired it was absolutely the right thing to do because when the sunlight seeped across the room, I felt better. More real.

'Hangover begone!' I said.

'Are you talking to me?' said Yorke.

'Blatantly not!'

Now the dust became visible and the room was full of sparkling jewels, hanging in the air. I stared at the glinting dust. Ephemeral forms, captured in minuscule particles, drifting on currents of air. So beautiful!

And the night had been dispersed by the day, and now everything shone. For a moment I was not remotely disconcerted. At all.

I put the paper carefully back on the desk. It was a coincidence. Or, I had seen the frills in Solete's room, the other day. My unconscious mind had absorbed them. I was jumping to conclusions!

'Sorry,' I said. 'Sorry, I just – I didn't sleep well last night.'

He looked at me and opened his mouth, as if he was about to say something. Then he closed it again.

We stood in silence, with the dust drifting between us.

'So what do you actually do in here?' I said. Trying to change the subject.

He smiled and said, 'I work on Light, and colour.'

'Like Robert Grosseteste?'

'You've read his work?'

'Yes,' I said. 'Well, especially *De Colore*.'

'I also work on Xenophanes, for example,' he said. 'In the sixth century BC, he said there were only three colours in the rainbow: purple, greenish yellow, red. He believed that everything that exists must always have existed, otherwise it cannot exist at all. And he believed the earth itself is infinite, just as it reaches into infinity. Like a rainbow, in a sense. Everything therefore has neither an end nor a beginning.'

'So what?' I said.

He shrugged. 'Homer called the rainbow triple-hued. No one ever said the rainbow had seven colours, until Isaac Newton divided it thus in the 17th century. Red, Orange, Yellow, Green, Blue, Indigo, Violet. But Newton even admitted that he was not very good at differentiating one colour from another. Originally he thought there were five colours in the spectrum – Red, Yellow, Green, Blue and Violet. Then he included Orange and Indigo, because he wanted his numbers to tally with the seven spheres, the seven notes of the musical scale, the sephiroth, the mystical significance of the number seven. It was a symbolic adjustment to reality. We make them all the time.'

'Tactless, in the circumstances, to talk about reality, wouldn't you say?'

He looked at me and smiled. 'Seven,' he said. 'The great arches of the ancient world. All creation encompassed. The single version of reality. Newton thought reality *was* light. Therefore, it had to be divided into seven as well. But this was plainly an imposition. Completely new.'

I remembered, ages ago, his question.

'Light,' he said. 'Rainbows. How many colours does a rainbow have?'

'You,' I was saying. 'Henges. Druids. Rainbows! You're an expert. Another one!'

He looked bashful. In response, I was angry. 'Why phone at midnight, that was the beginning of all this!' I said. 'A normal hour! Just a reasonable time of the night!'

'Sorry,' he said.

'Do you even know where you are? You're nowhere! That's where!'

I was adamant. But of course, it's illogical. If you're standing there, refusing to accept that a reality is real, then there's not much point making any assertions at all. Your assertions are, presumably, part of the unreality and therefore not real either. So you're back to the beginning.

'Well,' said Yorke. A flock of birds shrieked across the quad, heading towards Port Meadow. 'Do you want to go?'

'To the priests?'

'The Quantum realm, yes.'

Now we both aimed at a full recovery. 'If you've the time?' he said, politely.

'Yes, that would be good,' I said.

So we walked into the burnished city. The light was dazzling, though the air was cold. Frozen puddles glinted in the sun. The buildings looked whitewashed, standing against the blue sky. Tourists were being herded around the square, and at the top of one of the colleges I saw them progressing carefully along a parapet to admire the view.

I had seen it all, just the night before, in a dream.

'At least, I thought it was a dream,' I said.

'Everything OK?' said Yorke. Hands in his pockets, disturbing the line of his already crumpled suit.

'Rich, coming from you,' I said. 'Since when have you been a barometer of normality?'

'What, coming from me?'

'Then I shouldn't have taken tea, with those freaks, who freaked me so,' I said.

'Which freaks? There have been so many.'

'It's not even fair. I've led a blameless life. I've never been one to experiment. I've maintained what I felt was a steady and incremental path through life. Nothing out of the ordinary. Even when my father died, I never went off the rails. Solete saw that. He knew! And to send me to the fucking chrysanthemum people, it was a mean trick.'

'He didn't send you. Who sent you?'

'The mechanical magicians, but he sent me to them in the first place. Or Port did. By way of that freak Cassavetes. It was a trap!'

'You're tired. Overwrought.'

'Didn't I once say that to you?'

He paused and looked across at me, as we moved among the perpetual motion of the street, with the tourists surging onwards and people clutching phones to their faces, and the glittering pools of frozen water. At a college, an old wooden door creaked open, affording us a glimpse of a frost-white quad, students moving slowly in their halcyon enclave, carrying books.

'The quantum physicists have a theory,' Anthony said. 'Solete argued with them. About Light.'

'In what way?'

'In his own shifting and peculiar way.' He shrugged. I realised, too late, that he was making a joke.

We crossed the Parkland in silence. Shades and shadows and – I was thinking that we always make adjustments. People vanish, and yet, we continue, we assimilate impossible events. We call them normality even though they are madness indeed! I was thinking that I had strayed perhaps from ordinary reality but – still – the sun was shining in the usual way, and Anthony was not exactly reassuring but he was, at least, continuous. He was wearing one of his studiously crumpled suits and he was walking swiftly.

We passed over Nightingale Bridge and continued along the banks of the Cherwell, as it ran towards the Isis. The tendril trees were gleaming white and the frosted grass shone as if it had been scattered with diamonds. Then the greater river swallowed the smaller, and the moment was commemorated by nothing much, just a swirl of water, before the Isis flowed on, to the city of London, and the ocean.

The towpath was full of people who were happy again, their mood salvaged. The advent of the sun had relieved the tension. Though it was a little gusty, and the water was curdled by the wind, that was definitely preferable to torrid mist. A man walking a dog stepped aside to let us pass. We thanked him profusely. Then we all walked on again.

'How old are you?' I said to Yorke.

'Why?'

'I don't mean to be personal.'

'No, you achieved that already.'

I looked across at him. He was smiling. We were both sustaining an equable mood. I said, 'I just meant, are you married? Do you have children?'

'Yes, a daughter. Rosie. Very sweet. She's six. She lives in New York, with her mother.'

'You're divorced?'

'Yes. I didn't manage things well. I was penurious. I was clearly culpable. And the mother, well, she's very successful. Professor of Cultural Studies at NYU. A real – you know – Fucker.'

'So, when do you see your daughter?'

'Oh, I fly over, once a month. I can't afford more. And then, we talk a lot, over the web. So I see her. She sees me. It's clearly not ideal.' He looked completely crushed. 'If anything, it's quite dreadful.'

We kept walking. Another pause seeped across the banks and threatened to consume us once again. His wife had dumped him, and taken their child away. Now he saw the kid growing up, as a series of pixels, buzzed across the Atlantic. Bands of light.

'It's my fault,' he said. 'She tried. They both did, in fact.'

'You're being too hard on yourself,' I said. 'I mean, quite possibly. No doubt there's blame on both sides. Not the kid, I'm sure. But both sides of the adult equation, I mean.' I stopped, thinking at this point it was better to pause. Lest I offend.

Sometimes silence is less dangerous than speech.

This seemed to be one of those times.

We approached another estimable building. This one was a technocratic slab. It looked like a silver bird that had stuck its beak into the ground. Or, as Priddy said, a crashed aeroplane, nose-down. Its sloping sides were full of blank windows, reflecting the sky. Around it was a car park, filled with shiny cars.

A sign at the door said: 'Quantum Futures.'

'More prophets,' I said.

'I haven't met any prophets,' said Yorke. 'At all.'

'You need to drink the tea.'

Here the numerical realm was worshipped. That much was evident from the moment we arrived. We were hovering in the technocratic entrance hall, waiting for the receptionist to come back with orders from our host. They had put up screens everywhere, with scientist-heads speaking inaudibly. Then one of the scientist heads seemed to launch itself from the screen and appear beside me. Once again, I measured my impressions. I told myself that people do not descend from screens. Clearly they had filmed him earlier, and now the real version, the non-digital version, was standing beside me, with his hand out. He was wearing a t-shirt with numbers inscribed on it, and he had long silver hair. He introduced himself as Aubrey Land.

He was accompanied by another man, who was smooth and scalped by time, and said his name was Caspar Overson.

I asked Land about the numbers on his chest.

'An equation,' he said. 'Here –

$$\oint \vec{E} \cdot \hat{n}\, dA = \frac{1}{\epsilon_0} \sum Q_{in}$$

$$\oint \vec{B} \cdot \hat{n}\, dA = 0$$

$$\oint \vec{E} \cdot d\vec{l} = -\frac{d}{dt} \int \vec{B} \cdot \hat{n}\, dA$$

$$\oint \vec{B} \cdot d\vec{l} = \mu_0 \left[\sum I_{in} + \epsilon_0 \frac{d}{dt} \int \vec{E} \cdot \hat{n}\, dA \right]$$

It was one form of Maxwell's equations describing the relationship between the electric and magnetic fields. This was what Land explained, and then he said, 'If you want to, you deploy vector calculus on these equations, and then you eliminate B and thus you arrive at –

$$\left(\nabla^2 - \mu\epsilon \frac{\partial^2}{\partial t^2} \right) \vec{E} = \vec{0}$$

As he spoke, he pressed a button on a small device he was holding, and the equation appeared on the screen behind him.

'That's clever,' I said.

'Effectively, Maxwell thought light was a wave,' said Land.

'And is it?' said Yorke.

That prompted a flurry of smiles. They beamed, because the question was clearly in some way humorous. Yorke didn't smile. We walked, then, along a silver corridor. Everything was made of chrome, except the walls, which were covered in these screens, with prophet freaks enunciating silently. Secrets so esoteric we couldn't hear them.

Overson was walking ahead of us, looking shiny. Land was silver bright and he told us that Light is a wave according to Maxwell. And what was, is. So, the equations indicate that light is a wave.

'If you believe them at all,' said Yorke.

Time-smoothed Overson took up the refrain, as we walked into a shimmering laboratory, where there was a practical particle accelerator and a time crusher and a universe expander and then something else, that I was told

was a chair. I could sit here, without being projected across
the ethersphere and exploded into photons. I sat, quietly,
while Land said that there were rival theories that light is
a particle. Or, made up of particles. Streams of particles,
and thus we imagine light as dust floating in rays, again. I
thought of Alhazen, with his clouds of shining dust, and
I thought of a great desert, and drifting clouds of fiery dust,
settling on aged books. And the library at Alexandria,
burning to the ground, smoke clouds pluming across the
desert.

Here everything was sterile and if particles were permitted at all they were controlled and placed in an accelerator
and then –

Accelerated –

One had to assume.

Land seemed to be saying, 'experimental evidence'. We
nodded. Of course. Aristotle didn't need it. Bacon loved
it. The historic photo-electric effect, he added. This shows
that the wave model of light is not always sufficient.

'The nice equations on your t-shirt?' said Yorke. Amidst
the silver, he was more pallid than ever. He pushed back
his faded blond hair. He looked suddenly exhausted.

Land glanced at his chest. I noticed his hand was
clenched, like a claw. Some minor genetic deficiency, or the
asperities of age.

'When we say particles, or photons, we just mean things.
Light can be thought of as a load of individual things,'
said Land.

'Dust?' I said.

'These light things have energy that depends on the wavelength and so if you call the things photons then a brighter light just produces more photons per second.'

'Is light a particle or a wave or a collection of things?' I said.

'Really,' said Overson. 'The thing is. It depends on how it's feeling.'

'Light is mutable. Like everything else,' said Land.

'Why call it one thing or the other then?' said Yorke.

'We don't,' said Land. 'Here we favour a multipartite particle model of thing-dom.'

'Watch,' said Overson.

We watched, and Overson pressed a button on a small device he was holding, and the screen ahead flickered and changed, and the computer started spilling out Arabic. Except I realised it wasn't Arabic at all. Numbers not words. I had forgotten again.

$$\vec{p} = m\vec{v}$$

'But this might be wrong,' said Land. 'Do you see?'

Because it is not the spell to disperse shadows?

لالظإلا تايفيك

I wanted to explain, that this must be why it was not correct, at least potentially. But Overson was speaking again, and as he spoke he sweated, so he glinted with a sheen of animal heat and light – 'You might favour this model instead, you see.'

The screen said:

$$\vec{p} = \frac{m\vec{v}}{\sqrt{1 - \dfrac{v^2}{c^2}}}$$

'Relativistic momentum,' said Overson.

There was also a gravitational model of light, he added. So the screen illuminated another spell.

$$\vec{F}_{\text{grav}} = m\vec{g}$$
$$\vec{g} = <0, -9.8, 0> \text{ N/kg}$$

'But this is Wrong,' said the Over-priest and so when he smeared his forehead with his hand the screen changed and now it said:

$$F_{\text{grav}} = -G\frac{m_1 m_2}{r^2}\hat{r}$$

I fear I may have mixed up all the spells. In that case, what would occur? The world would run backwards. The path of the light ray would turn around. 'Could this occur?' I said.

They looked at me as if this was not the question I was meant to ask. What, then, was the question I *was* meant to ask?

'Solete came here a lot,' said Overson. 'He was a good man. A bit sceptical, and he called quanta little atomies, which is technically incorrect.'

'Why did he do that?' said Yorke.

'His point was that the word is not the thing. At one level, that's all fine. But the word, not-thing though it is, is also riddled with extant associations. If you use atomies then you are confusing everyone. There are separate things called atoms, of course. But Solete meant atomies in the sense of Leucippus, i.e. the smallest thing. So quanta were the smallest thing. Solete refused the later use of the word. He wasn't a scientist, of course.'

He was a man. And such a man – 'And so, he came and – did he say anything about the *Field Guide*?' said Yorke.

'Yes, of course. He came and conducted interviews. And he was interested in where the thing stopped and the rest of the world began. Where the edge of the atomie resides. If you can even find it. Why there, and not there, etc.?' said Land.

I was reeling slightly from the shock of the spell-casting, and now – Overson summoned another spell –

$$ih\frac{\partial \Psi}{\partial t} = -\frac{h^2}{2m}\frac{\partial^2 \Psi}{\partial x^2} + V(x)\Psi(x,t) \equiv \hat{H}\Psi(x,t)$$

'Schrodinger,' he said. 'Ψ is the wave function.'

'It looks like a vase,' I said. 'On a plinth. Or like the staff of Osiris. The pinecone. Does it have a cone fundamental?'

'No,' said Overson. But he was in denial. 'Psi, in Greek, or Ψ, is the twenty-third letter of the Greek alphabet. It has a numerical value of 700. The origins of the letter are completely uncertain, and it may or may not have been part of the Phoenician alphabet. Early on it looked like a chicken foot. But not now. Now it's curved and more beautiful. It was continued into the Algiz rune of the Elder Futhark. There it's a chicken foot, again. In quantum physics it's always a wave function. But it can denote the paranormal, as well. In a completely different discipline.'

'Your symbol is a paranormal symbol?' I said.

'Yes, but that's a different constituency entirely,' said Overson. 'I mean, it can also represent the rare nucleotide pseudouridilic acid, if you're really being a stickler. That's biochemistry. Or, in Astronomy, it represents the planet Neptune.'

'Why Neptune?' I said.

'As in the trident?' said Yorke.

'Triple spear. You use it to fight off negativity,' said Overson. 'But in physics you just use it to get the slightest sense of where you might find the thing, if there was a thing, at all. I mean, a light thing. A particle. Or an atomie, if you're Solete.'

'So the spell summons the thing, if there is a thing to summon,' I said. 'What if there isn't?'

'If you trap the thing in a box, a one-dimensional box, then you find the quant,' said Land. 'But you need a box. Otherwise, no.'

'The box in Solete's room,' I said. 'It was empty, but he wrote my name on the lid.'

'Well,' said Overson. 'There you are!'

'He was trapping the thing, if it could be trapped?' I said. 'But perhaps it couldn't. And how do you tell?'

Oh! said Overson. It was quite difficult to tell. Anything at all. The quant was not entirely the thing. Or the particle was not the quant. And you have to go up or down a staircase. You can't linger between the steps. So, this is true for a light thing in a box. It can only be there or there. You need a confined space, if not an actual box.

'But you can linger between the steps,' I said. 'Can't you? On the staircase, I mean, you pause, one foot aloft, and you wonder – should I go back. Or forward?'

'A photon is not a ball,' said Land. 'It is a thing, and light is quantised, and a photon is not and never shall be a neat little ball of light.'

'At one level,' said Overson. 'And really, at the most significant level, none of this makes any sense. At all.'

Anthony and I shook our heads politely, as if to say, we were sure it did really. But they weren't cast down anyway.

'Sense is relative,' said Land.

'The antiphotonists are far too worried about these things. They want to ban the word photon altogether. It is too old. On the base of plain ageism and for other more tenable reasons, they are intrinsically opposed. Radiation is not constituted of particles, that's absurd too, they say,' said Overson.

'It's just another form of extremism,' said Land.

'But what, actually, is Light made of?' said Anthony. 'Or, failing that, what would it be appropriate to refer to, when speaking about Light?'

'Einstein spent fifty years thinking about this stuff and realised he still couldn't answer the question: "What are light quanta?" He added that people who think they know what they are, are optimistic, but foolish,' said Land.

'And the speed of light is not even constant,' said Overson.

'It's been speeding up, and now it's started to slow down,' said Land.

'What happens when it slows down?' said Anthony.

'Nothing to you,' said Overson.

Then the screen changed and did this —

Ψ Ψ Ψ Ψ Ψ Ψ Ψ Ψ Ψ Ψ Ψ Ψ Ψ Ψ Ψ Ψ Ψ Ψ Ψ Ψ
Ψ Ψ Ψ Ψ Ψ Ψ Ψ Ψ Ψ Ψ Ψ Ψ Ψ Ψ Ψ Ψ Ψ Ψ Ψ Ψ
Ψ Ψ Ψ Ψ Ψ Ψ Ψ Ψ Ψ Ψ Ψ Ψ Ψ Ψ Ψ Ψ Ψ Ψ Ψ Ψ
Ψ Ψ Ψ Ψ Ψ Ψ Ψ Ψ Ψ Ψ Ψ Ψ Ψ Ψ Ψ Ψ Ψ Ψ Ψ Ψ

Then I realised that light was made of quanta things, and each thing quanta was shaped like this —

I saw the Ψ dust shining in the Ψ light. For all the sterility of the room, the Ψ dust swirled and shone. So beautiful, so Ψ. And the Ψ was also the Ψ of Osiris, and the Ψ of the Pope and the Ψ of Bacchus. And the middle prong extended until it formed a pinecone.

Of course, I shivered. The pineal cone of inner light!

Anthony was unseeing and he looked through the Ψ dust and yet he saw nothing of the Ψ. I felt disappointed and then I saw the dust was hovering around his head, as if it was emanating Ψ within him. Around him the Ψ. And Overson looked at me and cocked his head to one side, as if to say,

You have seen the Ψ.

'You have no idea where the *Field Guide* might be?'
Anthony was saying. 'None at all?'

'In the double slit experiment,' said Overson, quite
calmly, 'there are always two possibilities. The photons go
through both available slits, and so there are always two
worlds, if you are a photon.'

'Two possibilities is fine,' said Anthony. 'At the moment,
this thing could be anywhere.'

'But according to the way of logical trivium, you could
equally go one of three ways, if you want,' said Overson.

'I could?' said Anthony. 'I doubt that.'

'I mean, in general. Philosophically. The mythical
numbers are never even, are they? 3, 5, 7. They are odd.
The trinity. The spear. The trivium.'

'Which is what?' I said.

'Three paths cohere into one,' said Overson, smiling
happily. 'It's the classical route to knowledge. But there's
always the option to reverse it and develop something else
– entirely.'

I was left staring at him, in a certain amount of wonder.
The room whirred with mechanistic fervour, as if the particle smasher and the time inverter wanted to goad the priests
into a confession. The hum was in my head, it was consid-
erable. As the hum got louder, the photons, maligned and
even, to some, unreal, were being divided through two slits
as usual and then suddenly they went through not two slits
but three . . . The double slit experiment was transformed,
and became the triple slit, and photons did not merely go
two ways and through two slits but now and suddenly
Reality divided into THREE.

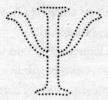

The photon trinity was among us and each event in time had not two but three possibilities –

But all three were part of the same sole possibility.

As we left Land and Overson I saw them nodding at me. Overson had one last piece of advice. I saw him sidling towards me. He said, 'You might consider it as a microcosm, instead.'

'Consider what?' I asked. I was even furious. Everything was asymmetrical. It was completely outrageous!

'The *Field Guide*,' he said, patiently. He put out his hand. 'I'd like to be of more help, if I can.'

'But can you?' I said.

'Think of it as a thing, not a book. That was what I was trying to say.'

'But a book is a thing,' I said.

'I simply mean, detach yourself from the notion of a perfect text. Try to find something altogether more – Ψ.'

'Are you speaking on the basis of knowledge?' I said. 'Anyway, how would something be more – Ψ?'

Overson laughed, as if this was a foolish question, and walked away.

◊ ◊ ◊

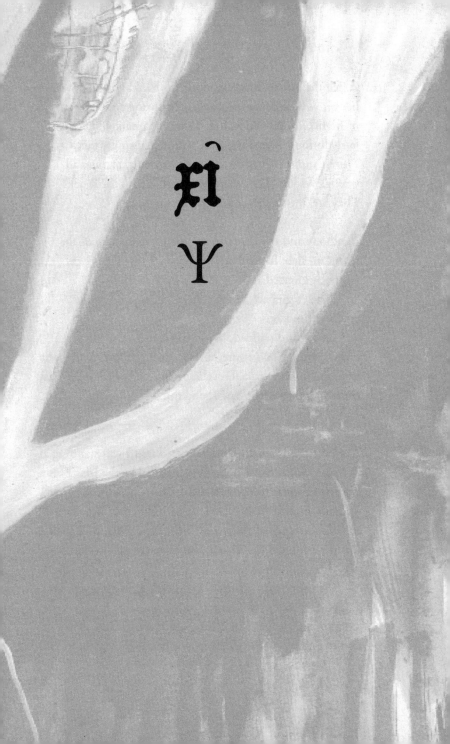

I felt the breeze shivering along the bank, tousling the hedgerows. Birds moved above, measuring circular paths of flight. Round and round – I was adamant and even fairly furious. Phenomena! Madness! An empty box. Things vanish. They don't fall apart at all, that was all wrong. Wrong! They vanish instead. That's the shock. They are, then they are not. An empty box!

Anthony and I were standing under the shadow of the quantum slab. It was hard to know what to say. Then, Anthony glanced at his watch.

'I have to go back to the college,' he said. 'Another student. I'm late.'

I smiled and nodded. What else could I do? He was always coming and going, this shivering elusive man! I was hoping for some crucial revelation but he just said, 'At least the mist has receded, that's good thing.'

'Of course,' I said. 'Yes.'

As I watched him go, I remembered that I was standing at the point where the Cherwell is engulfed by the Isis. This perturbed me as well. Why did the Isis drink the Cherwell and not the other way round? Why didn't they become a further river, called Acheron, or the New Nile, or Themis? Besides, why did the Ψ look like three rivers flowing into one? Or one river dividing into three? Where was the third river? Dust photons swirled and then I didn't know what to do. The water was shining in the sunlight. People were even rowing little boats, calling out to each other, their voices drifting on the air. Someone nearly dropped a punt pole, and laughed joyfully. I was beside the river with the traffic thrumming past me in its ordinary reassuring way. There were joggers passing me, looking healthy and purposeful. They were relieved, the sun had dispersed the mist and now the day was salvaged. At least for them!

I thought for a moment that I would just keep walking around the rivers and around the city until something occurred to me. But what would occur to me? The sun shone, as if some fetid branch of fate was trying to convince me it was all OK. I didn't believe the symbolic urgings of the weather. I kept thinking, surely if I just try one more time, I'll manage to solve the thing. I was completely convinced for a moment that I could still find this single final thing, and even the *Field Guide*, if I just made more of an effort. I had to find something, and put it in the box. Solete had left me alluring emptiness – and of course, what else do you do with emptiness? You fill it!

Just one thing. I only had to be resolute, or at least altogether more Ψ. With this in mind, I started walking along the banks of the Isis. Around me were clouds of dust, each particle illuminated by the sun, like buzzing particles of fire. They were falling from the skies, fiery dust, and I put up my hands to waft them away. I walked upstream for a while, as the weir curdled the river and roared, and further along as the cows splashed in the shallows and turned their faces towards me, and the sun boiled beneath the horizon, staining the sky red, and now the clouds were bruised and purple. Long slow shadows seeped across the fields. The city succumbed to dusk. I had reached a familiar boat. The deceptively neat sign – and there before me was – Cassavetes.

'Ah,' I said. I wasn't entirely pleased to see her. 'You again!'

'You have to stop,' she said. She was brandishing a boathook in a way that made me quite nervous. 'Just stop now! Remember the distinction!'

'What distinction?'

Without clarifying her terms in any way at all, Cassavetes slapped me round the face with the boathook and I fell into the freezing river.

It seemed astoundingly inhospitable. My cheek was burning with pain as I fell and then I got lashed with gelid water. As I descended into the depths, I tried to cry out, 'WHY?' But I was too cold to speak and besides my mouth was full of oily scum. Deep down, and the depths were so turgid, I couldn't see at all, though I opened my eyes and tried to look. Then it was so impossibly cold that I just wanted to get to the surface as quickly as possible, so I started kicking my legs frantically, and struggling upwards, as if I was climbing a ladder, and the gelid water bore down on me and seemed to draw me down again, so I kicked harder and harder –

I emerged into the sunlight, wheezing and coughing up river phlegm. My vision blurred, I saw Cassavetes looming above me. Because there was no other way out of the river, I dragged myself onto the mooring rope and fell shivering across the deck of her boat.

'Why the hell did you just throw me in the river?' I said, when I could speak again.

She was drenched in shadows, an unfathomable expression in her shadowed eyes. As I struggled to my feet I was trying to tell her that it wasn't my fault. Any of it. The

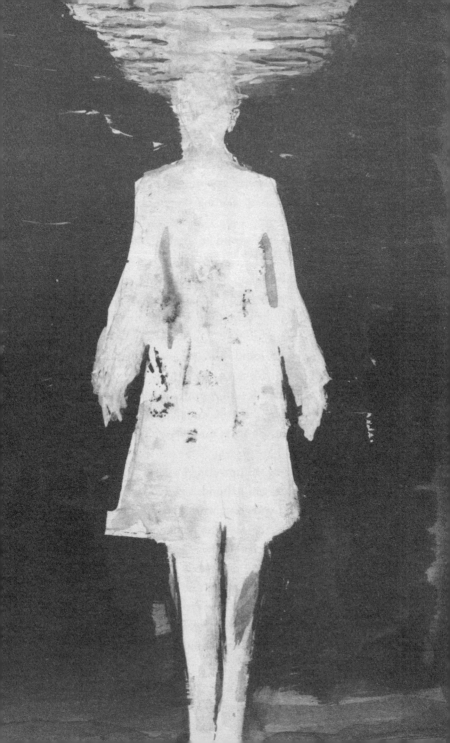

premature death of Hypatia, the confusion of the present. The shadows that were spreading. I wanted to tell her, but I was coughing too hard.

'You needed a ducking, you fool,' she said. 'What the hell have you been doing?'

'I've been — er — reading,' I said, dragging my weary body upright. Oily water pouring from my clothes, pooling on the deck. 'And meeting experts on reality. And, er, drinking tea.'

'Hopeless! Solete would be appalled, the way you've conducted yourself!'

'That's totally unfair! I'm simply trying to understand — '

'There is nothing to understand! You need to snap out of it! Get a fucking grip! Or, lose your grip on foolish things!'

'Well, which?' I said. Shivering and about to throw up. 'Which is it? Grip or not grip?'

'Stop gripping the wrong things! You have the wrong grip on the wrong things! Cast it all off! You'll send yourself mad, if you try to eat everything. Stop eating the universe!'

'I'm not eating the universe,' I said. It was madness, to be debating this, while shuddering in a pool of murky river water. Still, if I was going mad, I assumed I should keep moving, because there was no point going mad while being berated for my descent into madness by someone who was half-mad herself. So I jumped off the boat, and nearly fell back into the river again, tore my hands and knees scrambling onto the side and even as Cassavetes called me back I started running as fast as I could. *I will not be mad!* I cried out. I was sodden and much assailed by the cold and I was shivering, and spitting out protestations to the air, and a few people did look vaguely askance, but still, they were polite and they didn't want to hurt my feelings. They tactfully averted their gaze as I passed, dripping and fulminating and occasionally saying, 'The druid! She's a druid! And yet! I must not succumb!'

Dark figures everywhere. Dusty old shadows of the gargoyles above. The towers, casting a long line of black-ness. The grimy shadow-stained rivers. Onwards, to the shadowy ocean. Darkness made the city even stranger. Things seemed partial, there were intermissions, or I was shuddering with the cold and kept fading out. Despite all that, I thought I had to get back to Mesopotamia. I had to get out of the cold. I couldn't go back to my house – too far. I couldn't go to the college because the gargoyles leered – that was completely illogical. I passed Folly Bridge where Roger Bacon once sat in his tower, manipulating shadows, and then I saw the silhouette of Aristotle Hall so I thought of Locke and his dreams of white rooms, the celestial beyond, I almost succumbed to such enticing blankness. I heard the splash of oars on the river, and drifted into alert-ness again, I saw people moving alongside me, and I nodded towards them, even as they recoiled. I raved and squeaked around the edge of Aristotle Meadow, looking up at high blank windows, experiencing tremors of uncertainty, while I thought the fabric of the ordinary might disperse and reveal – something deep and ancient and formidable –

I shook that off again!

Nightingale Tower was pointing to the sky. I ran over to the door and hammered for admission. Only the porter's voice, asking what the hell I wanted.

'Depths of the night,' he said, informatively.

'Yes! Precisely!' I said. 'As soon as you see – Yorke – will you tell him? I'm going to Mesopotamia. Can't wait, or I'll freeze! Will you pass the message on?'

I didn't wait for an answer. Instead, I started running along the old henge, the humming all below me, around me. I got to the Parkland, coughing violently. I saw people moving under the trees, embodied memories, shadow-forms. I heard the rustling of old tired voices, or it was the wind-blown leaves skittering in circles on the path. The bridge arched its slippery back, and I almost fell, I was so damp and frozen and my hands had seized up entirely. I was so sad about the dead and I missed Solete. I missed my father more. I wanted to wail lamentations to the darkness. The black river below, the light fading entirely and when I passed into the shadows of the trees, I could barely see at all. I expected any moment that something, someone, would come, I was on the island, and I felt tendril roots below me, tripping me, so I stumbled, lost my balance, landed hard. Birds fluttering their wings above me, cascading into the trees. Again, I dragged myself up and thought, there's nothing to worry about! For some reason, you are wet, but that's not so bad. Soon, you'll be warm. At least dry. I ran into Solete's house and turned on

all the lights. Shadows receding, like snakes coiling into
the undergrowth. A flicker of something, I dismissed it, a
flicker of consciousness, dream matter, wafting, shadow
strands. In the living room I found a coat and a blanket,
and then I walked around the house, trying to warm
myself up, shuddering and moaning.

I was disoriented by the cold, and by much else besides,
but it seemed as if I had descended into a limbo state,
something that was neither sanity nor madness, reality nor
unreality. Something further along, or beyond entirely. I
kept trying to get back to one side, or the other. And yet,
I was adrift, I was far beyond the consoling parameters
of normality. But that was an illusion, I thought. The
biggest one of all! Reality − whatever the hell is around
you − doesn't fall into neat little categories − Light/Shadow.
Right/Wrong. Good/Evil. Dead/Alive. Reality is aligned
somehow with Light but you don't know what light is and
no one else does either. Whatever they pretend! However
many equations they thrust upon you! So therefore reality is
multiple and even still unknowable − and you seek to bind
it and confine it at your peril. And yet, you keep trying!
You want the thing, the single thing! The grail! And yet,
reality is myriad and legion. And − you are destined to fail.

It has failed and yet I am glad.

Even as I wondered at − everything − I became aware that
Robert Grosseteste was sitting beside me, wearing one of
his great clerical gowns and nodding in sympathy. Then I
was relieved, because if this was the final region of insanity
and the great shadow then it was kindly and quite familiar.
Really Grosseteste spoke in the most beautiful and gentle

voice, and he explained that later I would see the constel-
lations of the lesser realm. I was trying to ask him if he
minded about being so constitutionally and entirely wrong,
so much of the time, and perhaps always, but he ignored
me and stood up. He even walked away and so I hurried
along to keep up with him, as he went along the corridor,
towards the pinecone. The swoosh of clerical robes, on the
slate slabs.

As we approached, Grosseteste said to me, conversa-
tionally, 'The drawing of an eye. Have you seen Platter's
anatomical treatise of 1583, for example?'

I tried to explain that I had not.

'Look at the human eye according to Platter. Of course,
he enumerates it. Or rather with letters of the alphabet,
he denotes the relative parts. The crystalline humour, the
vitreous humour, the aqueous humour, and so on. But the
important thing is that Platter's eye is an inverted pinecone,
with its scales closed. It needs the Light to open it up.'

'Light opens the pinecone?' I said.

'Light permits you to see.'

Then he was drunk by the shadows and everything
changed again.

o o o

XII

The Rainbow
and the Halo

This time I really woke with a start. I was so cold, my teeth were chattering. 'Solete?' I said. I was huddled in a thick blanket and I was still wet. I sneezed several times, and coughed so hard my ribs began to ache. I was certainly feverish, and as my eyes adjusted to the dark I saw — a scene of shadows — Alhazen, Grosseteste, and Bacon — but they receded now, and took their leave. The last to go was Solete. He was wearing his hat, stooping a little as he went. I tried to call him back, but he drifted slowly away.

I was in Solete's house, in his cold living room. It seemed I had slept on the sofa. I had no idea how I had arrived here, I was struggling to regain any ordinary sense of continuity. Something had jumped. I was sweaty and cold then hot. I stumbled to my feet, aware that I could barely move, and tried to draw the curtains. It was that shady period, before dawn. The moon was dwindling, but the sun had not yet risen. The shadows were long, and the shores of the river looked eerie and silver-white.

I turned back to the ascetic room, the picture above the mantelpiece. The shabby sofa. I was wondering what to do, when Anthony entered, along with Petrovka and O'Donovan. Petrovka was elegant as ever in deep noir and O'Donovan had gone for another strident clash of colours. Another meaningful tie, which nonetheless I failed to interpret. He was shaking his head at me, expressing mild pity.

'What happened to you? Have you just arrived?'

Anthony interrupted, 'The porter hammered on my door at five a.m. He said you sounded dreadfully agitated, and you were heading for the Cherwell. I assume he thought you were about to throw yourself in.'

'No no, Cassavetes did that already,' I said. 'Well, strictly speaking, that was a different river. But, same principle.'

That made Petrovka shake her head as well. They started ministering warm clothes, blankets, more blankets, warm drinks. There was a long interlude while they were kind and I sweated and shivered. Everyone kept saying it would be fine. It was so reassuring, this general chorus of optimism, that I started to forget the impossible events of the night. In the daylight realm, we reassert ourselves, we say, 'This can be' and, 'This cannot be.' Diligently, I applied myself. They were helping me along, Petrovka and O'Donovan, while Anthony stood back, looking – uncertain. But that was his thing, I began to realise. No such feelings of doubt attached themselves to Petrovka. 'You've been under such a lot of strain,' she said, with conviction. That was probable, but then, what about her? She was taut with overarching anxiety, and O'Donovan kept biting his fingers.

'Still looking?' I said.

'We live in hope,' said O'Donovan. He sat down on the sofa beside me, moving my blanket, tucking me in. I felt instantly aggrieved, that he was so fastidious and proximate. Petrovka sat in the armchair beside me, on the edge of her seat, as if she was waiting for something. Both of them had an urgent look about them. Anthony glanced towards me and smiled. I tried to smile back, but I was too feverish, and I shuddered instead.

'I filed all of Solete's leftover academic papers,'

O'Donovan was saying. 'Took forever. He was not exactly organised. Sasha and I thought we'd make a book of his essays,' he said. 'Just to serve the bastard right. A desperate measure but what else can we do?'

'You really mustn't defame him, in his own house,' said Anthony from the doorway.

'It's not his house anymore,' said O'Donovan.

'Anyway, our houses are never really our own,' said Petrovka.

O'Donovan went to make more coffee. Petrovka explained they were planning a memorial event. A few eminent professors. They would collate the essays. Drinks and vol au vents. Speeches. It would be supremely tasteful, of course.

'Of course,' said Anthony, nodding along.

'If you'd like to come, I'm sure Churchwood would be delighted,' said Petrovka, to me, and then she waved towards Anthony.

'So kind,' he murmured. 'I'm overjoyed.'

'Light,' I said. 'Rainbows. How many colours does a rainbow have?'

'Seven,' said Petrovka. 'Of course.'

'Of course,' said Anthony, with a slight smirk. 'Couldn't be more obvious.'

Now O'Donovan entered with coffee cups on a tray, like a perfect host. As he handed them around it seemed we had returned to quotidian reality. The reality to which Solete had failed to supply a guide. The reality he had not mapped. The stuff we should be sure of, but are not. Where we reside, while we reside anywhere.

Here.

I was certain, it had resumed. After a brief glitch, an anomaly, we were back to the usual. I would shake off this fever if I drank the coffee down, and stayed in bed for a week, and then I'd go back – all the way back – to the normal and usual – and the café – and I'd work harder. I'd stay in my box –

The box –

For Eliade –

Then, quite abruptly, I knew.

I walked into the whitewashed corridor, towards the pinecone. Anthony jumped up and followed me, and that made Petrovka and O'Donovan nervous, so they came along too, holding their coffee cups, as if we were all off to a staff meeting. 'What is it?' they said. I was just thinking how I might answer that reasonable question when we all saw that behind the pinecone was a door.

'Perspective,' I said. 'The pinecone – Platter's eye. Permits you to see. The thing we need to see is – '

That got Petrovka and O'Donovan really perturbed, they started tugging and heaving at the great plinth, shoving it around with a complete lack of decorum.

Then I opened the door.

In the dim light of a sputtering bulb, we walked along a corridor and then stood at the top of a staircase. We all went downwards, in silence, and walked in single file along a lower corridor. This was a surprising edifice, an elongated cellar, the walls shrill with damp. We arrived at a further door, and I pushed it open and turned on the light.

The cellar echoed, cavernously, and was almost empty. The room was circular, the roof was slightly domed. The smell was musty, aged. Yet the place was abandoned. A few scraps of paper were lying on the floor. There were a couple of old chests of drawers, but when I went to look inside them, they were full of dust and mildew.

'How extraordinary,' said O'Donovan, wandering around, peering up at the ceiling. 'The roof, of course, meets the ground above. Where does it come out? Is it that slightly curved bit, by the bridge? What the hell did they keep in here? Not wine, they were clerics, after all. Was it the icehouse?'

'Solete worked for years to plan his *Field Guide*,' I said.

'Oh God,' said O'Donovan.

'At first, like all those long-gone maniacs he aimed at crafting a definitive portrait of reality. A single representative version: The Truth. But then he realised, they were all completely wrong. Their collective error was that each maniac, a.k.a. authority of the past, genuinely believed that their particular bonkers theory would encapsulate all reality, all history. Solete understood that the fundamental flaw of such a system – and in this he surpassed Plato, Aristotle, Alhazen and Grosseteste – was himself. He could only make one guide to reality and it would be, not a representation of general reality, at all, but a representation of himself.'

'Nothing wrong with that,' said Petrovka.

'Oh for Christ's sake, tell me he wrote an account of his dilemmas, a diary, anything,' said O'Donovan.

Both of them were looking faintly appalled. But they were going to get much more appalled. We had hardly

begun. It was an empty room, and the walls were covered
with moss and fungus. Variegated and quite beautiful
fungus but still, it wasn't what they had expected. I thought
by now I should be able to explain things more clearly.
After everything I'd seen. And all the enunciators!

I said, 'Solete came to believe that the fundamental
mystery and central property of reality is light. We wake
to the morning each day, and we turn our faces to the
sun. We subsist within this field of light and colour.
And yet, the speed of light is not constant. Light is not
constant. Everything about it is bizarre and preposterous. The rainbow has three or four colours during the
whole of classical history. Then Newton says it has
five colours. Then he changes his mind, and says it has
seven. A visible force, as Bacon proposed. But visible in
completely different ways, depending on when you are.
Where you are. And fundamentally unknowable. And
yet, it is everything we see. Gradually it sent him over
the edge.'

'Bacon?' said Petrovka.

'Solete. He abandoned his plans. Perhaps he even went
mad. Slightly, or entirely. And he realised, the endeavour
was mad. Certainty was raging mad. He had been mad
all his life. You could say at the end of his life he was
more sane than he'd ever been. Depending on how you
see things.'

This made Petrovka very nervous. 'What do you mean,
abandoned his plans?'

'Instead, he made something,' I said. 'He got that madwoman Cassavetes to help him. And on that basis, of
being helped and even actually guided by a madwoman,

he made a thing, not a book. It was fundamentally – well, it was basically about – light.'

'Oh shit,' said O'Donovan. 'Fuck and shit.'

I looked across at Anthony and realised he was smiling. I had never seen him so jovial. The atmosphere of defeat had gone and suddenly he looked – almost – young. Not quite; he sustained a few traces of the average whipping that life metes out to almost everyone, but some of the creases and tangles had been smoothed away. In response to a cue I hadn't yet discerned, Anthony switched off the light, and the atmosphere of the room changed. The curved dome of the cellar had been adapted, and seven holes, of different sizes, had been inlaid. As we stood there, day was breaking beyond the cellar, and the natural light of the sun flared. Seven rays of light seeped through the holes, and clouds of dust floated along these beams of light.

'Naturally the main reference is to Solomon's seven pillars of wisdom,' said Anthony. I saw he was smiling, broadly by now. 'These signify the seven sephiroth of the supra-celestial world, which are the seven measures of the fabric of the celestial and inferior worlds, in which are contained the Ideas of all things both in the celestial and inferior worlds. This should be clear?'

I said it was completely clear as anything.

We all stood, watching the beams of light progress, and occasionally fade. When the sun went behind a cloud, shadows spread from the walls.

When the sun returned, the dust shone like fire.

As Alhazen had watched the dust floating along rays

of light, the contours of light becoming visible, so we stood, and watched. We watched with varying degrees of appreciation.

'Shining dust, oh fucking hell,' said O'Donovan. 'Dust shines. In the light. I mean, Christ alive?'

'I don't understand,' said Petrovka. 'What the hell was he even thinking?'

'There's nothing to understand,' I said. 'It's a *Field Guide to Reality*, made from light and shadows. There are seven beams of light, descending. But the dust never quite descends, it drifts. Each beam of light represents a moment in history. But, the point is, you have no idea which is which. They are completely interchangeable. Of course! Atomies! Bits of stuff! Particles! Things! Many things. So many, you lose track. Entirely.'

'Are you fucking joking?' said O'Donovan. 'Is this actually a joke?'

'You're the one, Patrick, who has spent so much time assuring us it was a joke, that Solete was the perfect trickster, and now you're claiming to be surprised?' said Petrovka.

'He became uncertain, he got stuck, a terrible idea for a scholar,' said O'Donovan. 'He went mad.'

'And I have been saying that, from the beginning,' said Petrovka. But she didn't look particularly pleased. She wandered across the floor, breaking through one of the rays of light, disturbing the clouds. O'Donovan followed her, but I noticed he stepped carefully around the rays. They went to look at the scraps. The broken drawers. They made a great noise dragging them open, then slamming them

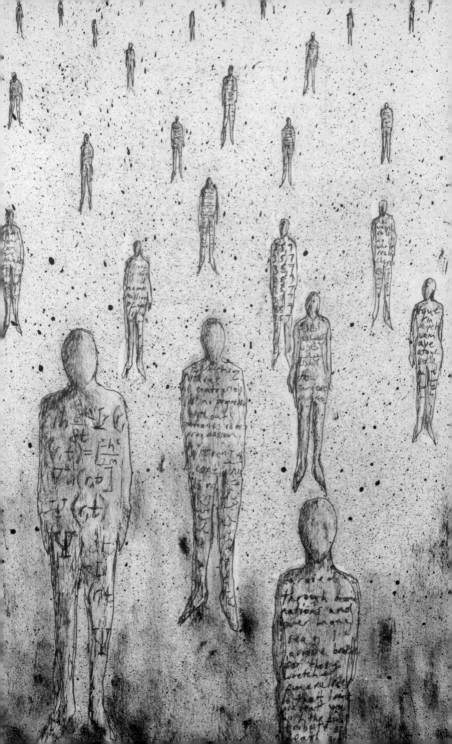

shut again. They were still hoping for something more tangible than dust.

A sorry affair, they were saying to each other.

The madness of a lone scholar. Well, a joke if you're feeling sick. Otherwise, a tragedy. Wouldn't you say? They continued along these lines as they slammed the drawers and picked through the scraps.

Of course, after the death of his wife – well, you don't necessarily recover, do you?

I heard O'Donovan saying, 'I pity the man, but still. Really!'

Meanwhile dust shone, reality shifted in line with the movement of clouds – light and shadow . . .

Unknown layers of time, immeasurable theories, and worlds, and realities, simultaneously represented and effaced.

O'Donovan lifted up his head and announced that he really had to go.

'It is time,' he said. 'If anything, it's overdue.'

'Me too,' said Petrovka.

She shook my hand, formally. O'Donovan joined in. He slapped me on the back, but he lacked his former zeal. 'It's a shame,' he said.

'We just wanted something complete,' said Petrovka.

'It is complete,' said Anthony, from the corner. 'How much more complete do you need?'

'You know what I mean, Anthony,' said Petrovka. 'And it's not funny, to stand around, pouring scorn.'

'Yes, get a fucking grip,' said O'Donovan, joining in. 'Otherwise, Churchwood will omit to renew your status.'

'Oh well,' said Anthony.

He was smiling to himself as O'Donovan abandoned the argument, and went to the door. They had the collection of essays to launch. Did I mind? 'We might just call it *A Field Guide to Reality*. A joke,' said O'Donovan. 'You know, Solete might have approved.'

'Do you mind?' said Petrovka.

I assured her that I really didn't mind. 'It's not even certain you have them anyway,' I explained, helpfully. 'There were other paths that may have vanished. At least, for a while.'

They nodded politely, and went upstairs.

For a while I heard the dull thud of their footsteps, and then there was silence. From O'Donovan and Petrovka, at least. Meanwhile Anthony was advancing another theory. 'He got tired of the ancient men of history, droning on. Bores with beards. Or cassocks. On and on. Anyway he erased them all. It was sabotage!'

'He said a lot of things.'

Anthony was fixed on his theory of academic immolation. He walked around, staring at the ceiling and muttering to himself.

Clouds of dust descended, and were flamed into brightness, and then faded again. Individual particles shone, and then became assimilated into a general cloud. I thought of Cassavetes and her muttered phrase. *Millions of years is the name . . . Otherwise said, millions of years is the name . . .* I thought about the vastness of measurable time, and those who dwell for a while within the linear frame. And then they are dispersed? Who knows?

Solete said he had failed. And yet – I wondered if this was merely the failure intrinsic to anything. All comes to dust. And he would have failed, harder and worse besides, if he had lied and created his mendacious, adamantine book. The more he discovered about reality, the more he understood that he could never define it, absolutely.

I thought of Petrovka and O'Donovan, publishing their collection, and staging their consolatory event. Giving speeches. Standing at the college pulpit and generally exonerating themselves. They would be severely rebuked but then, they'd forget all about this epoch. They would gain their desires.

The thing about Solete's chamber of dust, the main thing, was that it was incredibly beautiful. It gleamed and sparkled. It was the crazy beauty of particles that are normally invisible, of diaphaneity. We stood there, whirled around with remnants, and traces, and the abandoned schemes of Solete. He had gone mad, or he had perceived infinity. He had gathered everything, and lived within the richness of his contemplation and, in the end –

He refused his former truths, and went beyond them –

To the infinities of quanta, or atomies.

To the anonymous reaches of time and space.

o o o

Epilogue

Grosseteste walks along the dark and sinuous river, until he finds himself at Mesopotamia again. He slips into his study, and resumes.

Solete rises each morning, and goes towards the river, and waits.

Everything drifts backwards, and Grosseteste is in the draughty hall again, sitting with Bacon, Marsh, Duns Scotus and Ockham. Their shadows surge across the walls, as they lean towards the sputtering flames. They exchange their theories, as they always will. Bacon, the Marvellous Doctor, explains that reality is composed of shifting patterns of light.

And Aristotle is wrong.

Ockham dismisses universals, and the company starts, once more, in horror.

Poor Duns Scotus is buried alive again.

Some time later, the college hosts a grand tribute, and there are speeches in honour of Professor Solete. Bacon is in his tower, and Grosseteste dreams through the centuries. Alhazen is under house arrest, and mesmerised by flying dust.

The shadows loom and dance. As the moon rises, someone talks about diaphaneity. They all raise a glass to the memory of Solete. They are tactful, and pass swiftly over his theatre of dust. Instead they toast the publication of a final collection of Solete's essays, edited and introduced by Dr Sasha Petrovka and Dr Patrick O'Donovan. In respectful homage to Solete, these esteemed scholars have called the book *A Field Guide to Reality*.

Everyone applauds.

Standing among the crowd, I applaud too. When
O'Donovan approaches I say, 'This must be a truly exciting moment for you.'

He's formidably excited. But he understands the protocols; how formal and purposeful we must strive to become,
if we are to be believed. He smiles munificently and says,
'Of course! Sasha and I were just glad we could do justice
to Solete.'

'Of course,' I say. We stare at the assembled hordes,
fluttering their bony wings, slurping up college wine. The
great high velociraptor, Churchwood, bestowing honour
upon the worthy. Now I see Anthony, looking out of place
in another resolutely demolished suit, pushing his hair
away from his eyes. He wanders over, and O'Donovan
greets him with the kindly attitude of the victor, pats him
on the shoulder.

'Congratulations, I suppose,' says Anthony to
O'Donovan. Then he shrugs at me, to show he doesn't
mean it.

'I was just saying the same,' I say. To show I don't mean
it either. O'Donovan knows anyway, but he doesn't care.

'Look after yourselves,' he says, with immense bon-
homie. He grins widely, with his lopsided mouth. 'Don't
get into any scrapes.'

We assure him that it's highly unlikely. Then he saunters
away, to be heralded elsewhere.

'They lick the air,' says Anthony. 'When they speak.'

'They're happy at least.'

'The greatest irony of all,' he says. 'I mean, really, the
irony beyond the others – is that Solete created a theory

of the dissolution of theory. So, in a perverse way, it is a theory of everything. Just not the one they want.'

'Well, they've robustly misinterpreted it, and they're all very happy.'

'What about you?'

'Oh, yes, better now.'

'You don't need to lie.'

'I'm not. And you?'

He hesitates, then says, 'I got a job, in New York. Not at NYU. A small college out of town.'

'That's wonderful news,' I say, instead. The revised response. 'Of course, your daughter.'

'Of course, the fellows will be angry as hell,' he says, smiling. 'Churchwood especially. No doubt he was looking forward to firing me.'

'So, you've escaped, well done.'

'Thanks.'

We emphasise to each other that we'll be in touch. We're so eager to end on a simple, amiable note, that we barely say anything at all. So much has been hard to define. Of course, for a while, I was fairly lost. Still, I thank him for his help. We shake hands, formally. His hand is soft, and quite warm.

'Let me know, of course, if you're ever – passing through,' he says.

'Passing through New York? It seems fairly unlikely.'

He laughs. 'Of course! Totally absurd. Well, then, it will never happen!'

Famous last words!

I watch him as he walks, for once quite slowly, across the room. His shoulders are slightly hunched, so he reminds me, a little, of Solete. But that's inevitable. At the door, he turns again, and nods to me. The light fading beyond the windows.

I wave back. Then he recedes.

In the moonlight, the hall is tinged with a silvery glow. As they depart, the guests look somehow tenuous, less permanent than they did before. They are smiling and talking and fading, at the same time.

The next morning, on 23 January 2016, a double rainbow is seen on Port Meadow, Oxford. It is formed of two vast arches, which span the sky. The feet of the arches are planted at the centre of the meadow, and rise beyond the medieval town. The colours are perfectly rendered: the brightness is overwhelming.

I wander through the crowd, admiring the bands of red, yellow-green and purple, the peripheral colours beyond. The crowd is in raptures; there are people holding phones to the sky, conveying images across the cyber-ether. After a while, a TV crew arrives, to film the gaudy munificent rainbows flickering in and out of focus. The sunlight surges and the colours are transcendently beautiful. The lower arch becomes clearer, more definite, and the higher resembles a halo. The sky beneath the lower arch is brighter than everywhere else. A TV presenter moves within the crowds, asking how they feel about the colours, the brightness. The doubleness.

'A path made by a messenger,' says one.

'Five colours.'
'Three.'
'Seven.'
'The snake, governing the realm of water.'
'Ayona'achartan.'
The interviewer smiles politely, and moves away.

I attempt the impossible, knowing I will fail. I try
to walk towards the end of one of the arches. But, of
course, it seems to recede as I approach. On earth, we see
the rainbow as a line, from one foot of the arch, to the
other foot. It rises, and falls, we think. Yet, from the sky,
from Bacon's flying machine, or if you suddenly became
omniscient and eternal, you would see that a rainbow is a
circle. A zero, the number of eternity. There is no end to a
rainbow, as there is no end to a circle. It's simply a matter
of perspective.

After a while, the sun dwindles and the colours fade.
A cry of disappointment issues from the crowd, as the
rainbows disperse. For a while afterwards, everyone stands
around, uneasy and bereft. Then, the crowd exhales with
joy, as both rainbows surge into focus again. Everything
resumes, and the TV presenters stand again in front of the
rainbows, talking about the properties of light.

A few people notice that a man in a monastic gown is also
staring up at the rainbows, and moving among the crowd.
His face is obscured by a hood, his robes are covered in
mud. But no one thinks much of him. They are distracted

by their enterprises in photography, by the beauty and strangeness above them.

Anyway, Oxford is full of freaks, and a man in a gown is hardly remarkable.

Now legions of birds rise from the meadow, and circle in the darkening sky, and the air is full of melancholy song. Flocks of geese rise slowly, their wings thudding heavily above the crowds. The sun dwindles, and the moon sails into the sky. The rainbows fade for the last time, and, far above, the circle flickers and disperses into the blackness of space.

The clouds are stained vermillion, and the first stars emerge — *millions and millions of years* —

The past returns, and glitters in the sky —

Grosseteste takes his leave. He walks along the river, and into the shadows again.

○ ○ ○

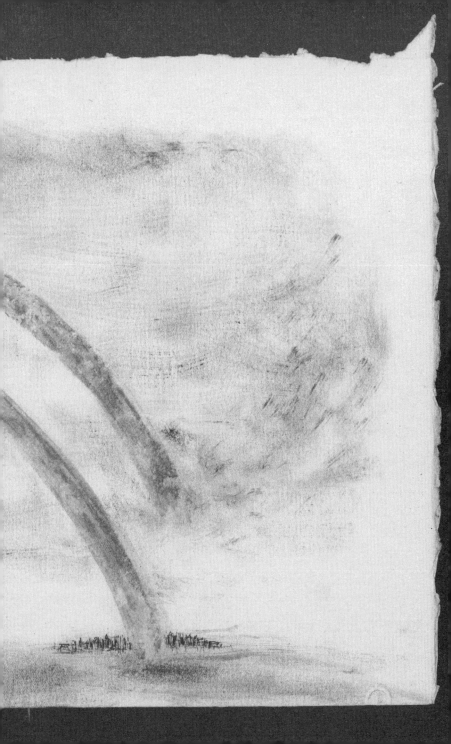

Acknowledgements

For his beautiful drawings, thanks to Oly Ralfe.

For sublime words and deeds, thanks to: Ai Weiwei, Hilary Lawson, Roger Penrose, Erik Rutherford, Miriam Toews, Angie Hobbs, Mary Midgley, Iain Sinclair, David Malone, A L Kennedy, Colin Thubron, Margreta de Grazia, Leo Carey, Robert Silvers, Peter Hacker, Sarah Chalfant, Iain McGilchrist, Rupert Sheldrake, Jill Purce, Julian Barbour, Yves Couder and Suzie Protière.

Thanks to the wise wizards: Jon Riley, Rose Tomaszewska, Georgina Difford, and Andrew Barker.

Love and thanks to BHDM, MK and BK, blissful surrealists, SCG, PD, DNyeG and ES, P⁄LM and BWM.

The esoteric properties of dust and the quest to fathom the mysteries of so⁄called reality have inspired countless philosophers, scientists and even novelists through the ages.

Onwards – Elsewhere!

About the author and illustrator

Joanna Kavenna is the author of *The Ice Museum*, *Inglorious* (which won the Orange Prize for New Writing), *The Birth of Love*, *Come to the Edge* and *A Field Guide to Reality*. Her writing has appeared in the *New Yorker*, *Guardian*, *Observer*, *Telegraph*, *Spectator*, *London Review of Books* and *New York Times* and she has held writing fellowships at St Antony's College Oxford and St John's College Cambridge. In 2011 she was named as one of the *Telegraph*'s 20 Writers Under 40 and in 2013 was listed as one of *Granta*'s Best of Young British Novelists. She lives in Oxfordshire.

Oly Ralfe is an artist, film-maker and musician. He collaborated with The Mighty Boosh and has recorded four music albums as Ralfe Band, including the soundtrack to the film *Bunny and the Bull*. His documentary films and music videos have won several awards.

A note on the typeface

This book is set in a typeface called Poliphilus and its accompanying italic, Blado. They were designed by the Monotype Design Studio and originally issued in 1923; this book uses digital versions produced some time later.

Poliphilus is based on the type cut by Francesco Griffo for Aldus Manutius to use in the edition of the *Hypnerotomachia Poliphili* published by the Aldine Press in Venice in 1499. Blado is based on the lettering of Ludovico Degli Arrighi *c.*1526.

The text in this book is set in 11.7 pt, on a 14.391 pt baseline grid. The reason for these seemingly awkward numbers is that the height of capital letters in 11.7 pt Poliphilus is equal to 1/78th of the full depth of the page; and 14.391 pt is 1/39th of the full depth of the page.

A Note on the Typeface